For The Love Of Family

The Bryar Family Saga

C J Bessell

Other Books in This Series

Pioneers of Burra

© Copyright 2021 C J Bessell

ISBN: 978-0-6451051-3-1

Dedicated to my amazing ancestors.

Chapter 1

Kooringa, 2ⁿᵈ February 1859

Alice held firmly to her father's arm. She'd never felt so nervous in her life and took a deep steadying breath. Not long now and she would be Mrs William Rowe.

It was only ten o'clock in the morning, but already the house was hot and stuffy. The voices of many people talking wafted through from the parlour, and all of a sudden her dress felt too tightly laced. She took several large gulps of air.

Her father looked down at her. "Are ye awright?"

"Aye, I'm fine Da," she said taking another breath. She was wearing her Sunday best dress, and her mother had managed to restrain her unruly dark curls into a bun. Several tendrils had since escaped, but Alice thought they looked rather pretty dangling down.

"Shall we go then?" he said opening the door and guiding her out into the hall.

They made their way through to the parlour which Maryann and Lizzie had decorated with garlands of ribbon. It was full to bursting with family and well-wishers, who all turned to admire her as they entered. She could see Will standing at the front of the parlour with Reverend Roberts. He had his back to her, which allowed her to admire him without him noticing. Her heart fluttered.

They walked slowly up to the Reverend and Will; he turned and smiled nervously at her. All of a sudden Alice felt very shy. She lowered her eyelashes and smiled demurely back at him.

"Do ye give this woman to be married?" asked Reverend Roberts.

"Aye," replied Richard removing Alice's hand from his arm and retreating to the back of the parlour.

A moment later both her hands were engulfed in Will's, and she turned to face him. He was wearing his best grey Sunday suit, and it looked like he'd trimmed his whiskers. His brown hair was parted down the middle and swept back on both sides. She thought he looked so handsome.

"Welcome Ladies and Gentlemen," said Reverend Roberts in his soft calming voice.

Even though he had spoken so quietly, the room immediately hushed. He looked around at the assembled people and then smiled warmly at Will and Alice.

Without any further preamble, he began. "Dearly beloved, we are gathered here in the sight of God, and in the face of this congregation, to join together this man and this woman in holy matrimony."

Alice found herself almost mesmerised by the calm monotones of Reverend Roberts. She must've drifted off because all of a sudden she became aware that the Reverend was looking at her enquiringly.

"Ah. I will," she replied.

He smiled at her with a rather bemused expression. "The ring?"

Will's brother Henry stepped forward and presented him with a thin gold band. Will took it and waited for the Reverend to continue.

"Repeat after me," he said "With this ring, I thee wed, with my body I thee worship, and with all my worldly goods I thee endow. In the Name of the Father, and of the Son, and the Holy Ghost."

Will obediently repeated the vow as he placed the ring on Alice's left finger. Alice's closest friend Louisa handed her a similar gold band, and she dutifully repeated the vows as she placed it on Will's finger. The Reverend droned on with more words about their future married life together, which Alice didn't pay much attention to.

The morning was starting to warm up and she thought by mid-afternoon it would be a real scorcher. She wished she'd thought to carry a fan with her.

Reverend Roberts placed his hand on the top of theirs which brought her back to the moment. "Those whom God hath joined together let no man put asunder."

The Reverend then spoke to the assembly. "Forasmuch as William and Alice have consented together in holy wedlock, and have witnessed the same afore God and this company, and thereto have given and pledged their troth either to the other. I pronounce that they be man and wife together. In the Name of the Father, and of the Son, and of the Holy Ghost. Amen."

"Amen," everyone murmured.

Will leaned down and kissed her, and she had to restrain herself from wrapping her arms about him and kissing him back. There would be time for that later. She had no intention of being at the centre of town gossip.

"If ye would both like to sign the register please," said Reverend Roberts indicating to a small table. The register was open at the appropriate page which had already been filled in with all the details of their marriage.

They both signed their names, and then the witnesses came over and signed theirs as well. Alice smiled as she looked at the register. It would the last time she would be Alice Bryar. Mrs Rowe, she mulled over in her mind and grinned more broadly.

Her mother was the first of the well-wishers to reach her side. She wrapped her in a warm hug. "Congratulations," she whispered in her ear. "I hope ye will be happy."

"Thank ye Ma. I'm sure we will."

Her father was next to congratulate her. "Ye are my first daughter married Alice, and I couldna be happier for ye," he said as he engulfed her in a tight embrace.

"Thank ye Da," she said hugging him in return. Will's father and mother were next in line to wish her well.

"We are so happy to have ye as our daughter," said Will's mother Elizabeth as she hung a good luck charm around her wrist. "I know ye will make him a fine wife."

"Thank ye," said Alice.

Will and Alice were kept busy for the next half an hour or so receiving congratulations and well wishes from their family and friends. Alice was almost relieved when her mother came by with a chilled drink for her and an ale for Will.

Finally, they were able to relax a little and enjoy the celebrations.

"Oh thank ye Ma."

Mary didn't stop. She had a houseful of guests to attend to and simply smiled at her daughter and continued on. Maryann and Lizzie came by next carrying trays of sandwiches and cakes. In no time at all the guests were all happily eating and drinking. Jenni was handing out chilled glasses of lemonade for those that wanted them, and even young Beth was busy. She was in charge of keeping two-year-old Esther out of trouble and minding her three-month-old baby sister Phillipa.

Alice tried to savour every moment, but time was flying by. In no time at all her mother was carrying the wedding cake into the parlour. She'd baked it herself and Maryann had decorated it with pink rosebuds made out of icing sugar. A sash of white tulle was tied around the base of it and fashioned into an elaborate bow. Mary placed the cake on the table along with a large kitchen knife which had a small pink ribbon tied around its handle.

"Attention everyone," said Richard clapping his hands together. "Will and Alice are going to cut their wedding cake."

Alice nervously picked up the knife and Will put one arm around her waist and his other hand on the knife with hers. Together they plunged the knife into the cake and everyone cheered. Alice undid the tulle ribbon from around the cake and cut a thin slice for herself and Will. She carefully placed it onto a small china plate and offered it to her husband first. He smiled at her and took a bite of the cake. Alice grinned back at him before having a mouthful of cake as well. It was delicious.

She was about to start slicing the cake into pieces for her guests when her mother came over and shooed her away. "I'll take care of that," she said taking the knife from her. "Ye need to go and change into your travelling outfit. Where's Louisa?"

"Right here Mrs Bryar," she said appearing out of nowhere. "Come on Alice I'll help ye." Taking her by the elbow she guided her out of the parlour towards the back bedroom. "Oh, it's been a wonderful day wouldn't ye say?"

"Oh aye. It's gone so fast though. I canna believe tis time for us to go already," said Alice as she allowed Louisa to help her out of her dress. She'd already laid out her travelling gown of pale blue cotton. Her mother's borrowed plaid shawl would complete the outfit. She put her cap on before admiring herself in the polished mirror. "What do ye think Louisa?"

"Ye look lovely, and I'm sure William will agree," said Louisa with a smile. "Speaking of such things, did ye see the way my brother was gawking at your sister Maryann?" She tucked several tendrils back under Alice's cap before standing back to admire her.

"No, I was too busy to notice. I think he's been courting her for some months though. At least he seems to be around here a lot."

"Oh he has," said Louisa knowingly. "I expect he'll be asking your father for her hand afore too long."

"Really? Do ye think it's that serious?"

'Aye, I know it is. At least I know Sam's head over heels for her. I dunna know how she feels about him though."

The soft sound of a baby crying reached Alice's ears. "I think I hear Phillipa crying," said Alice holding up her hand to quieten Louisa. "Beth was supposed to be minding her. Just wait here I'll go get her."

She hurried out of the room and returned a minute later cradling her young niece in her arms. "I expect she's hungry poor mite. We'll have to find Jenni."

Louisa leaned over her shoulder to look at the baby. "What's a matter with her?" she said aghast.

She was such a tiny baby and her head appeared to be twice the size it should be. She was wearing a tightly fitted cap, which was making her look even stranger. Her eyes seemed to be bulging and blue and red veins were visible through the skin stretched across her forehead.

Alice saw the horror on Louisa's face as she peered at the baby in her arms.

"She has water on the brain," replied Alice sighing. "Poor Tom and Jenni know she'll die afore she grows up. There's naught they can do."

"Aye. I've heard of it," said Louisa horrified. "Is there nothing that Doctor Morgan can do?"

"He does his best," said Alice jiggling Phillipa in her arms. "He's done some bloodletting which seems to help a bit, but he says he canna cure her."

"Oh, the poor wee mite. And that's so sad for ye brother and his wife."

"Aye."

The door opened and Jenni entered in a fluster. "Ye haven't seen Beth have ye? She's supposed to be watching Phillipa and I canna find either of them."

"Aye, well we have Phillipa," said Alice as she handed the baby over to her distraught mother. "I heard her crying just a few minutes ago and so I went to fetch her. I haven't seen Beth in a while though."

Jenni smiled broadly at the sight of her youngest. "Thank ye Alice, but ye should be out there saying farewell to your guests," she said as she gathered Phillipa into her arms. "They all be waiting for ye."

"Oh aye," replied Alice taking one last look in the mirror. "We lost track of the time."

Alice and Louisa departed for the parlour leaving Jenni to tend to Phillipa. Alice was overcome by shyness at the sight of everyone waiting for her. Her heart was hammering in her chest as she made her way over to Will's side. "I'm sorry we didna mean to be so long."

Will smiled warmly down at her. "Twas worth the wait Alice, ye look beautiful."

She blushed and smiled back at him. Oh, he was so handsome, and just being near him made her feel more at ease. They went around the circle of wedding guests together and bid each of them farewell. Will then put his arm around her waist and guided her out the front door. Their guests followed them out into the front garden and down the path where Henry was waiting for them with a horse and cart. Will helped her up onto the front seat before climbing aboard himself.

Alice waved farewell to her family as they started down the street. She would be spending her first night as a married woman at the Burra Hotel. Mrs Barker, God bless her, had given her and Will a room for the night as a wedding present. She glanced sideways at her new husband and tucked her hand under his arm. She sighed as he smiled down at her.

Chapter 2

Kooringa, 16th April 1859

The day was as gloomy and overcast as Tom's mood. The burial ground looked flat and bleak and he wished they could have buried her in the Churchyard. He cast his eyes towards the tiny coffin shrouded in a knitted shawl. He should have been prepared for this. They had known almost since the day she was born they would lose her. He just couldn't fathom how he was going to ease the ache in his heart.

He shifted his weight as he waited for Reverend Roberts to begin. His father stood nearby looking sober but relaxed. He'd buried five children and Tom thought he'd probably resigned himself to Phillipa's death months ago. As if reading his mind his father turned and moved closer to him.

"Twill get easier," he said putting his arm around his son's shoulders. "I know it doesna seem possible right now, but I swear it will."

Tom smiled grimly at him. "I know ye know Da, but I canna see how I will ever feel the same again," he said taking his eyes off the coffin. "I'm glad Jenni isn't here. She wouldna have been able to stand it."

Richard nodded knowingly. "Aye, tis no place for the womenfolk."

The Reverend Roberts stepped closer to the grave holding his bible in his clasped hands. He looked around at those gathered and cleared his throat. The murmuring voices silenced.

"We meet in the name of Jesus Christ, may grace and mercy be with you. As children of a loving heavenly Father, let us ask his forgiveness, for he is gentle and full of compassion," he said. "Let us commend Phillipa Bawden Bryar to the mercy of God."

A cool wind was blowing up from the creek and Tom cast his eyes to the sky. He hoped if it was going to rain it would wait until his daughter was buried. He shivered.

"We entrust Phillipa Bryar to your mercy in the name of Jesus our Lord, who reigns with you, now and forever. Amen."

"Amen," the men murmured in response.

Reverend Roberts spread his hands wide and continued. "We have entrusted Phillipa to God's mercy, and we now commit her body to the ground; earth to earth, ashes to ashes, dust to dust. Glory to the Father and to the Son and to the Holy Spirit. Amen."

"Amen," Tom murmured.

The Reverend then bowed his head and recited the Lord's Prayer. Tom spoke the words but found no consolation in them, and swallowed hard as they lowered the tiny coffin into the ground. He took off his coat and rolled up his sleeves. Picking up one of the shovels leaning against the carriage he joined his father and brother-in-law. Together they began shovelling dirt into the grave. It was so good to have something physical to do, and he found the rhythm soothing. Slowly the tension eased out of his muscles as he worked. Nothing would ease the pain in his heart, but the shared work went some way to calm him.

Once their work was done he laid a small posy of flowers from the garden on her grave. He stood there for a few minutes just thinking about her until his father put his hand on his shoulder.

"Come on, Tom we should go," he said. "Jenni and your mawther will be expecting us."

"Aye," he said looking at his father. "There's naught more we can do here."

.~.

Jenni hated the waiting. She picked idly at her mourning dress and wondered how much longer the men would be. The parlour was full of women and children, and yet she felt separate, disconnected. She sighed as she adjusted her hat.

Alice looked up from her knitting and smiled cautiously at her. She was only a couple of months off having her first child, and there was no disguising her growing belly. Jenni hated to be reminded of it. Not that she blamed Alice. Good God no, it wasn't her fault Phillipa had died. But still, she hated the constant reminder that Alice would have a baby in her arms soon and she did not.

"I'm hungry Mamma,' said Beth sidling up beside her. "When are we having dinner?"

Jenni sighed. "Soon sweetheart. We have to wait until your faather and Granfer come."

Mary overheard her granddaughter. "The bearns dunna have to wait, Jenni. I can feed them now if they're hungry."

"Awright. Thank ye," she said going back to her contemplation.

"Come on out to the kitchen and I'll fetch ye some soup and bread," said Mary taking Esther by the hand and beckoning to

Beth and Susan. "And maybe some cake if ye like."

"Thank ye, Grammer," said Beth happily skipping after her closely followed by Susan.

It had just started to drizzle with rain when the men arrived home from the burial. Tom looked tired and drained, and Jenni greeted him with a hug.

"Are ye awright?" she enquired. "Ye look exhausted."

"Aye. I'm fine," he said clasping her to him.

She knew he wasn't fine, but she didn't have any comforting words to give him. She didn't have any for herself either. She just held him close and hoped that conveyed how she felt.

He kissed her forehead and let her go. "Dunna worry."

Alice greeted her husband with a hug and was proudly showing him the booties she'd made. They appeared to be in a world all of their own.

"When's dinner," said young Richard grumbling. "I'm starving after all that digging."

His father ruffled his hair. "That's naught compared to the amount of ore you'll be hauling tomorrow."

Lizzie was busy putting out crockery and cutlery for dinner, and Maryann placed a large soup terrine on the table. Mary was right on her heels carrying a large platter of buttered bread.

"Come and eat while it's hot," said Mary to everyone as she sat down at the table. "The bearns already have theirs."

Maryann filled the bowls with piping hot soup and Lizzie placed them around the table. Everyone found themselves a seat and Tom sat down at the head of the table. As soon as everyone had settled he bowed his head in prayer and gave thanks. "Amen," he finally murmured.

Richard took a mouthful of soup and sighed. "Tis good soup Jenni."

She looked at him from across the table. "I didna make the soup. Tis Maryann that deserves the credit."

"Ah," he said grinning at his daughter. "I should have known."

"Aye, Da ye should've. Would ye like some bread?" said Maryann pushing the platter closer to her father. He took a slice and went on eating his soup.

"Tom, did ye hear the tut worker's pay was cut?" said Will swallowing a mouthful of soup. "Henry Ellis says he overhead some of them talking. Do ye know if it's true?"

21

"Aye it's true," replied Tom shaking his head. "I dunna know what they be thinking. There'll be no new pitches if they strike."

"Tom's right," said Richard grimly. "We'll be next. I reckon next Survey Day the Captain won't be offering us as much either."

"Ye dunna mean it?" said Will alarmed. "Do ye really think they'll pay us tributers less as well?"

"Stands to reason doesn't it?" said Richard dipping his bread into the soup. "And, what can we do about it? Unless we're prepared to pack up our families and move to Kapunda there's naught we can do. They've got us over a barrel, and they knows it."

Young Richard was listening to this conversation intently. He'd only been mining for a couple of months and knew better than to offer his opinion.

"Do ye have something to add Richard?" asked Richard looking at his son's inquisitive face.

He shook his head. "No Da...but, I dunna understand why they'd pay us less for the same pitch."

"Aye they must be making good profits," said Tom slurping his soup.

"However, tis all based on how much they can get for the ore."

"Aye," said Will nodding in agreement. "It depends on the price of copper, and if that goes down then so do our wages."

Young Richard nodded but didn't look any less confused.

"Dunna worry Richard. Twill be awright, we have a good pitch and I dunna think Captain Roach will deal with us unfairly," said Richard reaching for another slice of bread. "Eat your soup."

Chapter 3

Kooringa, 2nd September 1859

Alice felt numb. How could Will be dead? It didn't seem possible or even real. Barely a month ago she'd given birth to their beautiful daughter and named her after her own dear mother. She was the happiest she'd ever been. Everything had been so perfect. Now her father was kneeling before her telling her that her husband was dead?

She blinked and looked into his stricken face. "There must be some mistake Da," she said. "I saw Will this morning afore he went to the mine, he was fine." If only she could shake off this feeling of being someone else. She was talking to her father but it seemed like it wasn't her.

"There's no mistake Alice. I'm sorry to be the one to have to tell ye, but Will isna coming back," he said grasping her hands in an attempt to get her to understand. "I dunna know how he could have fallen. He must have missed his step."

"He fell?" she said tears welling in her eyes.

"Aye. I'm ever so sorry Alice." Even now, as he was telling her how her husband had fallen to his death, he wasn't too sure how it had happened.

Will had complained earlier that morning that his back was giving him a bit of trouble, but Richard hadn't paid much attention. The hard work of drilling the holes for blasting was done. They were now packing the holes with gunpowder and laying the first row of fuses.

Richard edged along the narrow plank. He could see Tom, Will and Henry Ellis ahead of him. They were all carefully tamping gunpowder into the drilled holes.

"Aah," said Will as he reached down for the fuse.

Richard looked up. "What's amiss?"

"Nothing. I just came over a bit dizzy."

Richard moved along the plank toward him. He thought he looked a bit pale. "Ye best go and take a few breaths of fresh air."

"Aye," he agreed. He edged to the end of the plank and headed off to the nearest air shaft.

Richard went back to preparing the holes for blasting. He would be glad when the job was done. It had taken far longer than he'd anticipated and he was anxious to finally get some ore out of this pitch. Not only had his new son-in-law joined his pare, but he now had young Richard working it as well. They'd need to haul more ore if they hoped to make a decent profit.

Will returned from the shaft and went back to work.

"Do ye feel better?" asked Richard concerned for his son-in-law.

"Aye I'm fine," said Will brushing off any concerns. "Dunna worry."

They had continued working for at least another hour when it happened. All Richard heard was the scraping of boots on wood and an alarmed gasp from Will. He must have lost his footing. Richard looked up just in time to see him tumble from the plank and plunge into the darkness below. Tom and Henry had noticed as well, they both looked at Richard horrified at what they'd just witnessed.

Richard's heart was hammering in his chest as he ran along the plank. He rushed to the end where their main ladder was leaning. He clambered down as fast as he could and ran to where Will was lying unmoving.

"Will, are ye awright?" he said in a panicked voice. He knew in his heart that he was not. Tom and Henry arrived on the scene and knelt beside him.

"Is he breathing Da?" asked Tom.

Blood was oozing from a cut behind his left ear and temple, but Richard could hear his heart beating when he placed his ear to his chest.

"Aye, he's alive. Come on help me get him onto a board and we'll get him to Doctor Mauran."

They managed to secure him to a plank and had carried him to the nearest plat where the ore was raised. By the time they got him to the Mine Hospital and in the care of Doctor Mauran, Richard was feeling ill. How was he going to explain to Alice that her husband had fallen and was seriously injured?

It didn't take Dr Mauran long to examine Will. He came out of the examination room with a grim expression on his face. "I'm sorry," he'd said. "You men have done your best, but Mr Rowe has succumbed to his injuries.."

At those words, Richard felt the earth shift beneath his feet. Tom, Henry and young Richard looked at him, horrified at the news. He sank into the nearest chair as he tried to make sense of what had happened.

He now found himself trying to explain to his daughter that her husband was dead. He could see that she wasn't comprehending it. He couldn't blame her for that. She was no doubt in shock at the news.

"If ye want to see him, Alice, I'll take ye," he said rising to his feet. "I dunna want ye to worry none though. I'll fetch your mawther and she can help ye pack a bag and ye and the bearn will come home with us."

Alice sat with her head in her hands ignoring her father. Tears welled in her eyes, but they wouldn't fall. The lump in her throat hurt and she swallowed hard. God, she didn't know what she was going to do. Her father waited patiently, but she knew she couldn't ignore him forever. No matter that Will was gone life would have to go on. She finally raised her head.

"I'll pack a bag for Mary and myself and we'll come home with ye," she said flatly. "I dunna want to stay here alone."

"Shall I fetch your Ma?"

"No. I can do it," she said finally getting out of her chair. "Twill not take long."

Richard waited patiently for her. He paced the small shabby parlour and ran his fingers through his hair. He wished Mary were here. He should've gone home and told her first, before coming here. He'd only had one thought on his mind though, to find his daughter and tell her as soon as he could.

He knew Tom and young Richard would be at his house by now, and no doubt everyone would know about the accident. He groaned and sat down in the chair that Alice had not long vacated.

Alice was true to her word and in no time at all came back into the parlour with her bag packed. She handed it to her father and went to get baby Mary. She woke up when Alice disturbed her and began to mew quietly. Alice fed and changed her before joining her father in the parlour.

Alice took a look around the home she'd shared with Will for such a short time. She knew she couldn't stay here. The Mine Company would want to rent it to one of its workers. She sighed and swallowed more tears that pricked the back of her eyes.

"I'm ready Da, let's go."

They walked to her parent's house in Church Street in silence. Alice was lost in her own thoughts and was grateful that her father seemed to understand. Her emotions were raw and she struggled to believe that Will was truly dead. If it was spoken aloud then it would be true. In her heart, she knew it to be so, but she wasn't anywhere near ready to accept it.

She was so glad to be going home to her family. They all gathered around and seemed to hold her and Mary in a warm hug. Her mother immediately took charge and she was so thankful. Arrangements for Will's funeral were made and Reverend Roberts offered her words of solace. He was so calm and kind. Over the next few weeks, Alice found the strength to face her loss and immersed herself in motherhood.

Chapter 4

Six weeks later Maryann married Samuel Gilbert. The entire Bryar family were still in mourning, and if Maryann could've changed her wedding date she would have. The arrangements had been made months before and the banns had been read. In the end, they had a simple wedding ceremony at the Church with their families attending.

There was no wedding breakfast afterwards. Maryann thought that would've been too much for her sister to bear. She and Sam went off by themselves to the Burra Hotel for supper and their first night together. It was a simple affair, but all Maryann was concerned with was getting married. She didn't need all the fuss.

Six months on the family was finally starting to recover from the loss of baby Phillipa and Alice's husband Will. In April Maryann went into labour with her first child. After a difficult birth lasting eighteen hours, her son was stillborn. They named him Samuel and buried him the following day with a simple ceremony conducted by Reverend Roberts. Maryann and Sam were devastated, and Tom and Jenni knew how they felt. However, the bad luck they'd endured for the past year appeared to be over.

In August Jenni gave birth to a fine and healthy boy. They were beside themselves with joy. Finally, they had a son. They named him Thomas Bawden Bryar after his father.

The following month Alice married for the second time. She and George Clark were married in a quiet ceremony at his home in Redruth. The whole family was present and Richard and Mary were so glad to see their eldest daughter happily married once again. George was a miner from Devon and joined the pare with Richard and his sons.

Towards the end of the year, copper was discovered at Wallaroo and the news spread quickly. Tom was so excited about the prospect of new opportunities.

"Da, I've heard that it might even rival the great Burra Burra Monster Mine," said Tom excitedly. "And I've heard a Captain Hughes has come to Burra looking for miners."

Richard took a mouthful of coffee and nodded his head. "Aye. What would ye have us do Tom? Pack up and move?"

Tom swallowed the mouthful of toast he'd only just bitten into. "Well, I dunna know about moving Da, but are ye not even a little bit interested? They may be paying better than here that's for sure."

"Aye, I hear they're paying much better," said young Richard. "Perhaps we should go Da."

"Well I dunna blame ye Richard, but Tom ye should know better," he said frowning at this sons. "We have our family to consider. We canna be packing up the women and bearns and moving. The mines are not long open, where do ye suggest we'd live?"

"We'd sort that out Da," said Tom dismissively. "Ye have to agree that we're getting paid less and less for our work. Why next Survey Day I hate to think what old Roach will be offering us."

George drank the last of his coffee before entering the fray. "I'm afraid I have to agree with your Da. Twould be a big upheaval for everyone."

Tom didn't pay George much heed. Everyone knew George was a cautious man. Tom thought he was too careful. Opportunities could be missed if they didn't act. "Well, I for one would like to know what Captain Hughes is offering."

Young Richard nodded in agreement. "I hear he's already got a hundred or so miners who've agreed to go."

Tom downed the last of his coffee. "They wouldna be going if he wasna offering them a better deal."

"Enough," said Richard at last rising from his chair. "We willna be getting paid at all if we dunna get to work." He kissed Mary who was clearing dishes from the table. "We may be late for supper tonight. Dunna worry, tis the last day of the contract and we need to haul a lot of ore today."

"Aye," she said handing him his bag into which she had packed pasties for them all. "Take care."

Talk of the newly opened mine at Wallaroo persisted. There were fears that Burra would be deserted by the end of the year if the exodus of miners continued unabated. Tom was anxious to be a part of it. The offering price for their pitch last Survey Day was a shilling less than the previous contract. Richard had accepted it, but Tom was unhappy with the situation.

"Ye canna be serious Da. A whole shilling less, and ye accepted it!" said an outraged Tom. "Why will ye not consider Wallaroo? I hear it even costs less to get the ore to the surface than it does here."

Young Richard seldom sided with Tom, but on this issue, he had to agree with him. "What if we just went down there and found out for ourselves?" he suggested.

After months of badgering Richard had to finally concede that his sons might be right. Rumours were rife that the Burra Mine was either not going to renew contracts, or that they would pay so low no one would bid on them. Richard also knew his sons and knew they wouldn't give up on the idea.

"Awright," he said glaring at them both. "But we canna just pack up and move without first finding out what's to do down at Wallaroo."

Tom looked at his father exasperated. "Da if we delay any longer we will miss our opportunity. Have ye not been reading the papers? New mines are opening up with good lodes, we should just go. Now." He rose from the table and walked anxiously to the window. He turned to face his father. "We can leave the women and bearns here until we've got somewhere for them to live."

"How do ye suggest we do that?" said Richard equally frustrated. "As soon as Captain Roach gets wind that we've gone he'll evict them. Then what will they do?"

"Surely George and Sam could take care of Ma and Jenni if that happened," put in young Richard. "I agree with Tom, we should go afore tis too late."

Richard sighed. "Awright. We'll have to talk to George and Sam, and your mawther. If we can come up with a plan then we'll go."

Tom's anxiety eased somewhat. He was confident George would stay in Burra and take care of Jenni and his mother. He thought Sam would want to come with them. Perhaps young Richard should stay behind as well until things were settled in Wallaroo.

A week later Richard gathered his entire family together to discuss the move to Wallaroo. He waited until they'd had supper before he told them why he needed to talk to them all.

"Some of ye already know that things are going from bad to worse here in Burra," he said. "There is opportunity to be had in Wallaroo, and if we can find a way to move there then I think we should."

There were various nods of agreement around the table. "There are some difficulties in moving," said Tom. "Mainly we'd need to get settled in Wallaroo afore ye womenfolk and bearns join us. The only available accommodation there at the moment is in tents."

Mary shuddered. "I willna leave my perfectly fine house to live in a tent."

"Nor will I," said Jenni horrified at the thought.

"We dunna expect ye to," said Richard calmly. "That's why we need to work out how we can do this, and not have ye living in a tent."

"Alice and I willna be moving to Wallaroo," said George. "I think people are rushing there under the mistaken idea that things will be better. But, some have returned."

Richard was not surprised by George's decision. He, like Tom, had expected it. "I respect your decision George," he said to his son-in-law. "Perhaps ye could help us by taking care of Jenni and the bearns until we get settled?"

"Aye I'd be more than happy to," he said reddening slightly. "I expect we'd have room for them to move in with us for a time."

"I thank ye, George," said Tom earnestly.

Jenni smiled warmly at him from across the table. "Ye are most kind George." She turned to Alice who was sitting beside her. "I hope it will not be too much trouble for ye Alice?"

"Not at all. I think we could fit enough beds for the girls in with Mary," she replied lightly. "What about Ma and Lizzie though? Have ye forgotten about them Da?"

"Not at all. Young Richard will remain behind and take care of them," he replied. "And I thought Maryann could move in with them as well so that Sam could come with us."

"But Da that's not fair," complained young Richard. "I dunna want to stay behind. Anyways, tis ye and Sam that have womenfolk to care for, not me."

"That's true," said Sam with a laugh "But ye are still a lad and have to do as your Da says. I thank ye, Richard, for staying and taking care of Maryann for me."

Young Richard glared at him. "I willna stay behind to take care of your wife for ye," he stated indignantly. "I'll be going to Wallaroo." He folded his arms defiantly and glowered at everyone.

"Ye will stay and take care of your mawther and sisters," said Richard with finality. "And I dunna want anymore argument from ye."

"So tis decided then," said Tom grinning. "As soon as I've got Jenni and the bearns settled we'll go."

"Aye," said Sam also grinning widely. "I canna wait to see it. I hear tell tis a fine mine with huge seams of ore."

Richard nodded. "Aye, tis decided. We'll have to store some furniture and household stuff seeing as we're putting four households into two. I'm sure it willna take long to get that sorted."

Young Richard was still sitting with arms folded glaring at everyone.

"Twill not be for long, son. In no time at all you'll be joining us in Wallaroo," said Richard trying to placate his youngest. "And besides we couldna do this if ye didna stay."

"Humph I suppose so," he begrudgingly agreed.

Chapter 5

Kooringa, February 1861

It was several weeks before Richard, Tom and Sam were ready to leave for Wallaroo. They stacked what furniture and household goods they could fit into the back room of Richard and Mary's house. Poor young Richard was reduced to sleeping in the corner, with the bulk of the room being used for storage.

Maryann moved into the other bedroom with Lizzie. She had only recently announced that she was expecting again. Everyone had their fingers crossed that her baby would arrive alive and well.

"I expect twill be several months afore we see each other again," Richard said hugging Mary close. "I canna tell ye how much I will miss ye." He kissed her affectionately. "I'll write ye as soon as we're settled."

Mary hugged her husband tight. They'd never been separated before, and she was apprehensive about what lay ahead. She was glad he had Tom and Sam to look out for him. She knew he was capable and still very fit for a man of fifty, but still, she was well aware they were not as young as they used to be.

"Write me as soon as ye can. I will worry until I hear from ye," she said letting him go. "And dunna worry about us. Young Richard and George will do a fine job of taking care of us all."

"Aye, I wouldna be going if I didna think that," he said giving her a final kiss.

"Time to go Da," said Tom coming in the front door. "John and I have loaded the trunk. ye just need your bag."

They'd packed the sea trunk with their mining tools and equipment. Not being too sure what would be available at Wallaroo, that included gunpowder and candles. They'd left enough supplies for Henry, George and young Richard who would be mining their pitch at Burra while they were gone. They'd also packed a few rudimentary cooking utensils and other household items. Hopefully, they wouldn't need to buy too much when they got there.

"Aye," replied Richard picking up his bag and taking a last look around. "Say goodbye to Lizzie for me."

"Aye I will," said Mary. It was only half-past five in the morning and there was no sign of Lizzie. She'd said goodbye to her father last night, although Mary knew that she'd hoped to be up early enough to see him off.

Sam and Maryann were in a tight embrace saying their final farewells. "Come on," said Tom slapping Sam on the back. "You'll see her again soon enough."

"Ah that's awright for ye," said Sam letting go of his wife. "Your wife isna expecting your first bearn."

"Aye tis true," he replied grinning at his brother-in-law. "Take care, Maryann." He gave his sister a quick hug before saying goodbye to his mother.

It was nearly six o'clock before they finally made it out the front door. John Duncan was waiting for them with his dray. He was around Tom's age with a mane of long dark hair which he wore tied back with a length of leather strap. Since copper was discovered at Wallaroo he'd been running a passenger service from Burra. He had enough room in his dray for several trunks and four passengers.

Richard put his bag in the back of the dray and climbed aboard. Tom and Sam climbed aboard as well and the three of them settled back in readiness for the journey ahead. At least it wasn't winter and unlikely to rain. Quite the opposite. The weather had been hot and dry for weeks and Richard thought it was likely to continue like that for a while yet. The sun wasn't yet up, but he expected the day to be hot.

John Duncan climbed up onto the driver's seat. "Are ye right to go then?" he asked swivelling in his seat to look at his passengers.

"Aye," replied Tom.

"Alright then." He turned his attention back to the horses and they were off. The men waved and called final farewell to Mary and Maryann who waved in return until they were out of sight.

It was about one hundred miles to Wallaroo via Port Wakefield. John had confidently told them that it would take three days. As they headed off Richard couldn't help but hope that the journey to Wallaroo would be easier than the one from Adelaide.

The first day's travel took them south from Burra to Black Springs and Mintaro. It was late afternoon when they arrived at Walter Catford's farmhouse at Stilly's Creek. His farm consisted of a well-built stone house, along with several barns and outbuildings. Richard was surprised to see such a house. Most farms they'd passed on the way had far simpler wooden huts with lean-to verandas.

"We'll be spending the night here. The accommodation is simple but clean," said John indicating to a sturdy looking timber building. "Mrs Catford will have prepared supper for us if ye like to head over to the main house. I'll just take care of the horses." He jumped down from the dray and started unhitching the horses.

Richard, Tom and Sam climbed down from the dray and Richard stretched his cramped back. The journey hadn't been too bad. The day had been hot but a steady breeze had made it bearable. Now that they'd stopped however the flies were buzzing around and sticking in his eyes.

"Damned flies," he complained waving his hands about. "Come on let's see if we can get some supper afore bed."

Tom and Sam grunted in agreement, equally happy to get inside and away from the flies. The three of them headed off towards the welcome relief of the homestead.

John woke them before daybreak the following morning. They dressed and following a hearty breakfast supplied by Mrs Catford they all climbed aboard the dray again. They hoped to make Port Wakefield before nightfall where John said they would pick up supplies. After a long hot day in the back of the dray, Richard sighed with relief when they stopped at

Henry Bowman's residence just south of Port Wakefield.

The house was a typical wooden structure with a wide shady veranda along the front. A huge peppercorn tree growing near the front shaded nearly the entire house. There was a barn out the back with a sagging roof badly in need of repair.

John climbed down from the dray. "We'll be staying here the night," he said indicating the barn. "ye probably will not care that the accommodation is a bit rough."

Richard climbed down from the dray and stretched. John was right. He couldn't care less how rough the beds were going to be. It would just be so nice to stretch out and relax. Henry Bowman provided them with a tasty supper of boiled potatoes and mutton. Following a couple of ales and slow conversation, Richard was falling asleep. He bid them all goodnight and headed for the barn.

The barn was warm and stuffy and smelled of hay and rotting manure. There were several beds to choose from, all of which were just sacks stuffed with straw with a thin blanket over the top. Richard lay down and apart from the straw sticking through the hessian sack and prickling him, he thought it could've been worse. In no time at all, he was asleep and snoring loudly.

The following morning they were once again up at daybreak. After a simple breakfast, they helped John load several water casks onto the back of the dray. Once the horses were hitched up they all climbed back onto the dray and they headed off on the last leg.

This proved to be the most dreary part of their journey. The day was hot with barely a breeze, and the treeless landscape was flat and dry. It was mainly open grassland with occasional areas of dusty scrub. There were no farms or other settlements and no fresh water to be had.

It was late in the afternoon when they got their first look at Wallaroo. Just past Hughe's woolshed, they could see the smoke from the engine house. Beyond which were rows of neat timber tenements and pine and calico tents. There were several stone buildings as well as a general store and post office. Quite a number of buildings were under construction including a hotel and several houses. On the whole, it was flat, hot and dusty.

"This is the only hotel in town," said John coming to a halt outside the Globe Inn. It was a low single-story building with a twin-gabled veranda along the front. "The proprietor's William Square. Tell him I sent ye."

Richard slowly climbed down from the dray. After days sitting on the narrow seat, every muscle felt cramped and sore. "Thank ye, John," said Richard grabbing hold of one end of the trunk. Tom took hold of the other end and they hauled it off the dray.

Sam grabbed the rest of their luggage and dropped it on the ground beside the trunk. "Aye thank ye, John."

"No worries," he replied climbing back onto the dray. "When ye get over to the mine, ask for Captain Hancock." He clicked the horses and went off down the street in a swirl of dust.

Richard was tired. It was hot and he was parched. "So how about we introduce ourselves to Mr Square and get settled in for the night?" he suggested picking up his portmanteau. "A pint or two would go down a treat as well."

Tom grinned at him. "Now you're talking Da."

Sam nodded. "Aye. The best idea you've had all day."

Chapter 6

Tom was up at daybreak the following morning. He was tired from the three day trip from Burra, and the accommodation at the Globe Inn had left him with a pain in his shoulder. Nonetheless, he was eager to start the day. Richard looked exhausted and had not had a good night's sleep.

"Tis awright for ye two young whippersnappers," he complained grumpily. "We'll see how ye feel when you're my age and spend three days in the back of a cart. I can hardly move. Every damn joint aches."

"Well, why don't ye go back to bed and Sam and I'll go and speak with Captain Hancock," said Tom trying to soothe his father. "I'm sure he'll be happy to give us a take on a pitch."

Richard took a mouthful of coffee. He grimaced at the bitter brew and scowled at his son. "I'm not going back to bed, and ye willna be going to the mine by yourselves," he said biting into his toast. "Ye will need me with ye."

Sam smiled behind his mug of coffee. "Aye. Your Da's right Tom. We'll be needing his help to get a good deal with the Captain."

Richard continued scowling at the two younger men, but seemed to relax somewhat when talk turned to home. "I'll have to write Jenni tonight and let her know we've arrived safe," said Tom finishing his breakfast.

"Aye. Maryann willna be happy with me if I dunna write her as well," said Sam. "What about you Richard? Is Mary expecting you to write?"

"Aye. She'll worry until she hears from us," replied Richard. "We'll all have to write letters home tonight. Here's hoping we have some good news for them."

Sam and Tom nodded in agreement. "Well, shall we get going then and find some good news for them," said Tom standing up from the table. "I for one canna wait to see the mine for myself."

The three of them headed out of the hotel and into the bright sunny morning. It was already warm and promised to be another hot dry day. They walked down the wide dusty street in the direction of the mine, looking at everything as they went.

Wallaroo was so new and raw and everywhere Tom looked was a hive of activity. He couldn't help but get caught up in the excitement of such a brash new place.

New copper discoveries were almost a weekly event, and shafts were being sunk at a rapid rate. Tom saw opportunity everywhere he looked. He hadn't realised until now just how stagnate Burra was because the South Australian Mining Association wouldn't release any land. Here, he could buy land and build a house of his own. He couldn't wait to write to Jenni and tell her that Wallaroo was all they'd hoped it would be.

It was only a short ten-minute walk to the mine, and Tom was anxious to see it. They passed the tents and a few outer buildings before they arrived at the mine site proper. It consisted of two shafts and one engine house. A large crusher was still under construction but nearing completion by the look of it. It was nothing like the size of the Burra operations, but Tom knew it wouldn't be too long before it would be. There were several large piles of ore, but Tom noticed there were no sorting sheds as yet.

"That looks like the mine office over there," said Richard pointing towards several stone buildings. Tom and Sam looked and nodded in agreement before striding off in that direction.

Richard opened the door and the three of them went inside. There was a tall burly looking man behind a wooden counter. He looked up when they entered and smiled. "Good morning to ye gentlemen, can we help ye?"

"We're looking to speak with Captain Hancock," said Richard walking up to the counter. "We hear he's the man to talk to about a pitch."

"Oh aye," replied the man. "He'll be back shortly. Have ye just arrived then?"

"Aye, just arrived from Burra yesterday. Tis our first day here in Wallaroo," said Richard and introduced the three of them.

"Well I be the head carpenter here, John Wickes is the name," he said shaking hands with them. "We've had a lot of folks come down from Burra, and we dunna have any houses for them as yet. Will ye be wanting accommodation then?"

"Well that depends," replied Richard warily. "If we can do a deal with the Captain, then aye, we'll be needing some accommodation."

"We'd be happy with a tent," put in Tom. "We dunna have any womenfolk with us as yet. We'll send for them if all goes well."

"Aye, well I can arrange a tent for ye, but I expect you'll want to speak with Captain Hancock first. He willna be long."

John Wickes was a fountain of information and was happy to tell them all about the mine and Wallaroo while they waited for the Captain to return. There was a shortage of water due to a lack of freshwater creeks or lakes in the vicinity. He recommended they buy their water from Captain Francis for two pence a bucket. His water distillery was the best according to Wickes.

"I reckon you'd still be able to get an allotment in Thomas or Hughes Street for less than twenty pounds," said John Wickes when they got onto the subject of land. "Ye should speak with Mr Alexander in the Land Office, he'll know what's available."

"Oh aye I'd be interested in that," said Tom enthusiastically. The prospect of having his own house was enough for him to make the move to Wallaroo. He knew Jenni would be just as excited about it as he was. "I'll definitely speak with Mr Alexander. Up in Burra we canna buy land or get our own place."

"Aye I've heard that," said Wickes. "Never fear gentlemen, here ye can buy some land and settle down proper like."

The door opened and a rather tall imposing man with a flowing beard entered the office. He removed his grey bell topper as he came in and noticed the three strangers. "Morning gentlemen," he greeted them. "Is Wickes assisting you?"

"Ah, Captain Hancock. Let me introduce Mr Bryar, his son and son-in-law Mr Gilbert. They've just arrived from Burra and are looking for work," said Wickes. "I told them ye would be able to help them."

"From Burra you say. Welcome gentlemen," said Captain Hancock. "I expect we should be able to assist you. Mr Hughes was recently in Burra, did you speak with him?"

"Aye my son did," replied Richard.

"That's right," said Tom. "I spoke with him. He said he was in need of experienced Cornish miners. Said he could offer us a pitch with better pay than we were getting at Burra."

"Yes I expect he did," said Captain Hancock with a smile. "Our next survey day is a month off, but I can offer you a couple of options. Firstly we could ask one of our current pares to take you on, or else you might be interested in taking on your own pitch. That would be at a set rate and wouldn't include subsist pay. Of course, you'd be free to bid as usual come survey day."

Richard nodded and took a moment to think through their options. Tom and Sam looked at him and waited. "Well, either option would suit us just fine Captain. Seeing as survey day is a ways off though, we'd be more than happy to join an existing pare until then. If they'll have us that is."

Captain Hancock nodded in agreement. "Well, I tell you what. I'll make some enquiries, and if you'd like to come back tomorrow afternoon I'll have an answer for you."

"Aye that sounds like a fine idea," said Richard. "We'll come back tomorrow afternoon then."

"Don't worry gentlemen. If none of the miners will take you on, I'll do you a fair deal on a pitch."

"Thank ye," replied Richard.

They left the mine office feeling optimistic that they'd secured work for the next month. Tom didn't mind the idea of living in a tent, but he was anxious about getting a house for Jenni and the bearns. They would remain in Burra until he had that sorted.

"How about we go by the Land Office," suggested Tom as they made their way back towards town. "I for one would like to find out if we can get some land for a house."

"Aye good idea," said Sam. "Tis one thing for me to live in a tent, but Maryann willna be coming until I've got her a house to live in. I'm missing her already."

Richard slapped him on the back and grinned. "Come on then, let's see if we can get ye a house."

Chapter 7

Kooringa, March 1861

Jenni heaved the last load of laundry into the basket and went to hang it out to dry. Alice was propping up the clothesline which was already loaded with washing.

"I hope that's the last load, Jenni." Alice sighed as she began pegging it onto the available line. "My back is killing me."

Jenni smiled at her. "Aye, tis the last load. Leave it, Alice, I'll hang this lot. Why don't ye go and see what the bearns are up to? They're awfully quiet."

Alice finished pegging the shift on the line and eagerly took Jenni's advice. "Awright, thank ye."

Jenni watched her head back into the house before continuing to peg the washing out. It wasn't yet noon but already the day was unseasonably warm. Jenni wiped the perspiration from her brow as she finished hanging the washing. She put the washing basket back in the wash house before heading into the house. It was so nice to get out of the hot sun, even though the house wasn't a lot cooler.

Seven-month-old Tommy was on the floor trying desperately to reach four-year-old Esther's blocks. She was managing to keep them just out of his reach as she piled them high.

She looked up at Jenni with her big dark eyes. "Look Mamma," she said pleased with herself. "No Tommy." She pushed his chubby hands away from her toppling tower just in time.

"Come on, leave your sister alone," said Jenni scooping Tommy up into her arms and kissing him. "We'll have to find ye something to play with."

"There's a letter there for ye Jenni. It looks like it's from Tom," said Alice trying to contain her wriggling daughter. "Stay still Mary."

"Down. Down," insisted eighteen-month-old Mary kicking her legs wildly.

"Stop it this minute," said an exasperated Alice. "I'm going to change her. The letter's on the table." She headed off to the bedroom with a now screeching Mary in her arms.

"Thank ye," Jenni called after her. She popped Tommy back down on the floor and grabbed the letter off the table. Since Tom had been gone he'd been writing to her almost weekly. After nearly two months though she was missing him like mad, and a letter every couple of weeks wasn't enough. She held the letter and hoped that it contained good news. Maybe he'd be sending for her and the bearns soon. She certainly hoped so. She ripped open the envelope and unfolded the creamy paper.

Wallaroo Mines
16th March, 1861

My Dearest Jenni,

I pray that you and the bearns are well and in good spirits. Rest assured that we are all enjoying the best of health down here.
We have secured an excellent pitch which should prove to be most profitable. The copper ore is plentiful and as the mine is less than twenty fathoms deep it is far cheaper for us to get it to the surface. Father is anxious for young Richard to join us, and so we are doing our utmost to find suitable lodgings. That is proving most difficult in the short term.

Jenni paused. Hmm, young Richard - he was becoming more disgruntled by the day. She was getting quite concerned about the way he was behaving. The last time she'd seen him he'd spent the entire evening ranting about how unfair it was. What concerned her most was that his ire was directed at her and Tom.

"Next time ye write Da, tell him to send Tom back here so as I can go to Wallaroo," said young Richard to his mother. "Tis Tom who should be here, not me."

"I will do no such thing, and ye will stop with this Richard," said Mary scowling at him. "We will all be in Wallaroo soon enough."

"Not soon enough for me. I'm not the one with a wife and bearns to care for. I should've gone with Da in the first place," he said glaring at Jenni. "Da always favours Tom afore me." He sat with his arms folded with his young face screwed into a frightful scowl.

Mary was exasperated with him. "That is not true and ye knows it. I dunna want to hear another word out of ye."

For a moment Jenni thought that was the end of it, for tonight at least. He was glaring at her from across the table and she tried to turn her attention away from him. She thought it best to say nothing and hope he'd get over it.

"Well ye better write to Tom and tell him to come back home, because I dunna care what ye say, I'm going to Wallaroo."

He rose from the table and stormed through the house and out the front door which he slammed loudly behind him.

"Dunna worry about him Jenni," said Lizzie as she cleared dishes from the table "He's all talk, he willna go to Wallaroo."

"I'm not so sure Lizzie. He seems awfully angry about being left behind, and he obviously blames me and Tom for it."

"Tis not your fault or Tom's, ye know that," said Mary sitting down beside Jenni. "He wouldna be behaving in such way if his faather was here."

"Aye he wouldna," put in Maryann. "The thing is he's only fourteen but he thinks he's a man."

"Well he isna acting like one," said Lizzie raising her eyebrows.

"Well I hope he willna hold this against Tom," said Jenni frowning. "I wouldna want this to come between them. They're brothers after all."

"Dunna worry Jenni," said Mary patting her on the arm. "Twill all be forgotten once we get to Wallaroo. I know my sons."

"Aye, I do hope ye are right."

Jenni's thoughts returned to the letter that she was clutching in her hands. Oh, she prayed to God young Richard would realise they'd had nothing to do with him staying in Kooringa. That had been his father's decision. She put all thoughts of young Richard aside and continued reading the letter.

I was most glad to receive your last letter, and your agreement that we should purchase land. To that end, I have secured an allotment in Hughes Street and have contracted a modest house to be built. It should be completed before winter sets in proper. I am missing you and the bearns something fearful, and cannot wait until we are reunited. Alas my dearest, that will not be until the house is completed. The only accommodation available here right now is under canvas.

Give my love and ongoing gratitude to Alice and George for taking care of you and the bearns. Hug them all for me and kiss the bearns. I'll write you again as soon as I have news.

Your ever-loving husband Tom.

Jenni sighed as she reread the letter. It would still be several months before they could be reunited. She'd hoped it would be sooner, but she knew they couldn't live in a tent with four bearns. At least they would have their own house, and she was excited at the prospect. In the meantime, they were all crammed in with George and Alice, but she was forever grateful for their kindness. Alice never made her feel like she was a burden or that it was any trouble for her to have them stay.

"Was it good news?" asked Alice coming back with a now quiet Mary by the hand.

"Aye," said Jenni. "They've got themselves a good pitch, and Tom's building us a house. Twill still be a while afore he sends for us though."

"Dunna worry. ye are most welcome to stay here with us for as long as ye need to," said Alice. "I'm only sorry that George and I willna be going. I dunna know what I will do when ye all leave."

Chapter 8

Kooringa, June 1861

Mary tucked her cloak in around herself. A weak wintery sun was peeking out between a few scudding clouds, but there was a chilly breeze blowing. She knew it was going to be cold travelling in the back of John Duncan's dray, but she prayed it wouldn't rain. The three-day journey south to Wallaroo would be miserable enough without rain.

Her eldest granddaughter Beth was sitting beside her wrapped in her own warm cloak. She would be making the trip with her, Maryann and young Richard. John Duncan didn't have enough room for all of them to travel together. His dray only had room for four passengers and their luggage. It had been decided that young Richard would accompany his mother, Maryann and Beth. The following week Henry Ellis would travel with Jenni, Lizzie and the rest of the bearns.

"Goodbye Grammer," said Susan as she clambered up onto the dray and then onto her grandmother's knee. "I miss you."

"I miss you too sweetheart," said Mary giving her a warm hug and a kiss. "I'll see you soon though."

"My turn," said Esther trying to shove Susan aside so that she could get onto Mary's knee. "Move Susan, tis my turn."

Reluctantly Susan got off her knee but didn't move any further away than she had to.

"Goodbye Grammer," said Esther giving her a big kiss.

"Goodbye, Esther. You be good for your mawther won't you?" said Mary hugging her close.

"Aye, I will."

"Come on down you two," said Lizzie. "Ye will see her again soon enough." She lifted Esther down onto the road, but Susan insisted on climbing down by herself. Lizzie smiled at her; she was such a tomboy.

Jenni reached up onto the cart and kissed her eldest daughter on the cheek. "Ye be good for Grammer and Aunty Maryann awright? We'll see ye next week."

"Aye. I'll be good Mamma," she replied unperturbed by all the fuss.

"Dunna worry Jenni, we'll take good care of her," said Mary seeing the tears welling in Jenni's eyes. "Twill only be a week and we'll be together again."

"Aye I know," said Jenni wiping the tears away with the back of her hand. "Tis just that we've never been apart afore. I know she'll be awright with ye."

Young Richard helped Maryann up onto her seat. She was only a couple of months off having her baby and her movements were becoming slow and awkward. "Thank ye, Richard." She sighed as she sat down opposite her mother. "I'll be glad when this bearn is born."

"Ye think that, but once the bearn comes you'll wish for the peace and quiet that ye have now," said Alice. She reached up and gave her mother one last kiss. "I am missing ye already Ma."

"And I am missing ye as well," said Mary. "I'll write ye with all the news as soon as we're settled."

"Thank ye," said Alice with tears in her eyes. "I dunna know when I'll see ye again though."

"Dunna worry Alice. I'll try and come for a visit afore too long."

The last member of the party to climb aboard was young Richard. He bid his sisters, Jenni and the bearns farewell before he settled himself next to Maryann. John Duncan gave the luggage one final check before climbing up onto the front seat. "Awright?" he queried.

"Aye," said young Richard. "Let's get going."

With a click of the reins, they went off down the street.

"Goodbye Grammer," yelled Susan waving frantically from the street.

"Goodbye," called Mary waving in return. She continued waving until they were out of sight. She sighed. They were embarking on a whole new chapter of their lives, one that would hopefully prove to be better for all of them. If only they weren't leaving George and Alice behind.

Once they'd cleared the outskirts of Kooringa the road became rutted and corrugated. The dray bumped along at a trot and Mary wished she'd thought to pack a cushion to sit on. The hard timber seat was most unforgiving. She'd have bruises on her behind before the day was out. She thought for a moment that she might sit on the heavy wool blanket that she'd brought with her. The cold breeze, however, convinced her otherwise. She unfolded it and wrapped it around Beth and herself. At least they would be warm.

"Do ye think our furniture will have arrived in Wallaroo by now?" asked Maryann raising her voice above the noise of the dray.

"Aye, it should have arrived two days ago," replied Mary. "I hope it's all arrived in one piece. I dunna entirely trust that Jimmy Bray."

The rest of their belongings and furniture had been loaded onto a bullock dray two weeks ago. Mary just hoped that Jimmy Bray could be trusted. She hadn't had much confidence in the way he'd stacked everything on board. He was about to tie down Richard's favourite chair when she'd stopped him.

"Jimmy, ye canna tie that rope around the legs of that chair," she'd said alarmed. "Twill be ruined afore ye get a mile down the road."

He stopped rope in hand and looked at her bemused. "She'll be right missus. ye don't want it to fall off do ye?" He went on wrapping the coarse rope around the legs of the chair and pulled it tight.

"Please, Jimmy. At least wrap something around the legs to protect them from rubbing on that rope," she'd said. The legs would be rubbed back to bare timber by the time they arrived in Wallaroo. She hurried back inside the house and came back out with a soft cotton sheet. "Here Jimmy, please wrap this around them first."

He'd rolled his eyes to heaven and groaned, but much to her relief had done as she'd asked. The rest of their furniture had been loaded in a similar fashion, and tied down with coarse thick rope. He'd then covered the entire load with large canvas tarps. Mary satisfied herself with the fact that at least their belongings would arrive dry.

The first day of their journey took them south to Stilly's Creek where they would be spending the night at the Catford's homestead. It was late afternoon when they arrived, and Mary was stiff and cold. She climbed down from the cart with some difficulty. Her joints had stiffened up after hours sitting in the one position. She stretched and stamped her feet as she tried to get her limbs to work.

"Are ye awright Grammer?" asked Beth frowning at her grandmother's behaviour.

"Aye, I'll be awright in a minute. Tis just my poor old joints."

"Oh," said Beth clambering down from the dray. She clearly had no idea what Mary was talking about.

"Head on into the house, Mrs Catford will be expecting us for supper," said John Duncan as he helped Maryann down. "I'll be along once I've taken care of the horses."

"I do hope Mrs Catford will make us some tea," said Maryann stretching her limbs and taking her mother by the arm. "I think we're both in need of something to warm us."

Young Richard and Beth seemed quite impervious to the cold as they marched ahead of them into the house. Mary wondered at the joys of youth as she struggled to get her legs to work. She almost dreaded the thought of another two days in the back of the dray.

Apart from the cold winds which chilled Mary's bones, the next two days of their journey were uneventful. Beth chatted almost incessantly and seemed to enjoy travelling. She was particularly excited when she spotted a mob of kangaroos crossing the road ahead of them. Mary suspected that she was enjoying being away from her younger sisters. She was acting so grown up.

Mary was thankful the rain had stayed off. Dark clouds had gathered on the morning of the third day, and she'd expected the heavens to open at any minute. However, they blew away to the east before dumping their load.

They arrived on the outskirts of Wallaroo late that afternoon. All four of them were anxious to take in all the sights of their new home. John Duncan took them down the main street, and Mary was delighted to see that there were so many buildings. She'd half expected the place to be a sea of tents. They continued down John Terrace before turning left at the Globe Inn. It was a wide street with newly built houses, and Mary wondered if one of them might be theirs. She didn't have to wonder for long as they turned another corner into Hughes Street. About halfway down the street, John pulled the dray up outside a small limestone house with a veranda along the front. It looked like a typical miner's cottage.

"Is this our house?" asked Mary. Her own house. She'd never imagined such a thing in her life and was so thrilled and excited at seeing it.

"Aye well I hope so," said John Duncan as he helped her down from the cart. "Tis the address I was given."

"Thank ye." There wasn't a front fence or even a path up to it, just a bit of worn dirt which led to the middle of the veranda. "I canna believe we have our own house."

Young Richard bounded up to the front door, opened it and disappeared inside. Mary and Maryann were still making their way towards the veranda when he reappeared.

"Aye, tis our place Ma," he said grinning widely. "All our furniture's in there."

Young Richard was closely followed by Sam. "Maryann," he exclaimed as he ran and swept her into his arms. "I canna believe tis truly ye." He hugged and kissed her and Maryann cried with joy.

"I have missed ye so much," cried Maryann, finally pulling out of his arms and looking at him. "Ye are looking very well, Sam. Twould appear Wallaroo suits ye."

"Aye well, I'm surprised, to be honest. I'm not much of a cook, and your Da's even worse. We've had naught but mutton and potatoes for near on a month now," he said distastefully. "I am so looking forward to ye cooking us a fine supper if ye are up to it."

"Well maybe not tonight," she replied wearily. "Ma and I are both cold and tired from our journey. I dunna care what we have for supper."

"Aye," said Mary in agreement as she stepped onto the veranda. "Dunna expect me to be cooking ye a fine supper either. I dunna care what we have so long as I dunna have to cook it."

Sam smiled at the women. "Well awright, twill be mutton again. Come inside, I've got the fire going so tis nice and warm

for ye," he said taking Maryann by the arm.
"Richard, why don't ye help John there with
the luggage while I get the womenfolk
settled?"

Mary stepped through the front door
and was immediately enveloped by the
warmth. She sighed as she removed her
cloak and looked around her new house.
There was a small entrance hallway with the
parlour leading off on the right-hand side.
On the other side was the main bedroom.
There was another bedroom off the hall and
a sleep-out at the back. Mary went through
to the kitchen, which was also located at the
back of the house next to the dining room.
There was a good-sized hearth and room for
her kitchen dresser and table. She opened
the back door and stepped out into the small
backyard. There was a covered porch to the
washhouse, otherwise, the yard was empty.
She'd have to get Richard to put in a
clothesline before too long.

She went back inside and through to
the parlour where Maryann and Sam were
waiting. "Tis so lovely, I never dreamed that
we'd have our own house," said Mary
smiling at them. "What about ye Sam? Are
ye building a house as well?"

"No, I dunna have enough money as
yet," he replied. "Richard said we could stay

with ye for a while until we get our own place. I hope ye dunna mind?"

Well, they would be crammed in thought, Mary. Then again, they'd lived under cramped conditions before, and as long as she had her family around her she didn't mind. "Twill be fine Sam, I dunna mind in the least."

Chapter 9

Wallaroo, June 1861

Tom paced the parlour anxiously looking out the window every thirty seconds or so. Jenni and the bearn's were arriving this afternoon and he could barely contain his growing excitement. The last few months being separated from them had been far harder than he could have imagined.

He hoped Jenni would be happy with the house he'd had built for them. It was a modest timber cottage with a tin roof. The front door opened directly into the parlour which had a small hall leading to the back of the house where the kitchen and two smaller bedrooms were. The main bedroom went directly off the parlour at the front. The washhouse was out the back and he'd installed a tank to catch rainwater.

He put another log on the fire which was already blazing in the front parlour. He wanted the house to be warm and cozy for Jenni. He looked out the front window again. There was still no sign of John Duncan and his dray. He sighed and sat down by the fire. He wished he could ease his growing tension. His leg was nervously jumping up and down and he ran his hands through his hair. God, he hated this waiting.

Half an hour later they had still not arrived and his anxiety was nearly driving him mad. He went to the window and looked out again, expecting that they would not be there. He was just turning away when some movement caught his eye. John Duncan's dray came to a halt in front of the house, and he could see Jenni wrapped in her cloak on the back seat.

"Thank God," he exclaimed out loud to himself before rushing out the front door to meet them.

Susan was climbing down from the dray and Henry Ellis was lifting Esther down when he arrived. "Henry, ye made it I see," he said clapping him on the back before taking Esther into his arms and hugging her close. "Hello, did ye miss me?"

"Aye, I missed ye Da," she said hugging him back.

He put her down and hugged Susan. "I've missed ye so much," he said kissing her.

"I missed ye too Da."

Lizzie climbed down from the dray and sighed with relief. "Tis so good to be here," she said hugging her brother. "Did Ma and Maryann arrive awright?"

"Aye. They were very tired but in fine spirits."

"Aye, and cold as well no doubt. I know how they feel."

He looked up at Jenni who was handing Tommy to Henry Ellis. He grinned at her before putting his hands around her waist and helping her down. He took her in his arms and hugged and kissed her.

"Oh, Jenni I have missed ye like mad."

She clung to him and kissed him in return. "Tis been too long Tom. I dunna want to be parted like that again."

"Aye. Dunna worry I willna be letting you and the bearns out of my sight again," he said earnestly. "I'm just so glad that ye are finally here, safe and sound."

"Here take your son and I'll get the luggage," said Henry handing Tommy to him. "Mind he's wet and in dire need of changing." He laughed as he went to help John with the bags.

"Oh great, thanks," said Tom holding his son at arm's length. Tommy took one look at this father and started to wriggle in displeasure. He held his arms out to his mother and started to cry.

"Oh dear, he doesna remember ye," said Jenni taking her son into her arms. "That's your Da. Do ye not remember?" He quieted as soon as he was in Jenni's arms and scowled at his father.

Tom was a little dismayed at his son's reaction. However, he consoled himself with the fact that the last few months apart must have seemed an eternity to his ten-month son. It was no wonder he didn't remember him.

"Come into the house Jenni, I've got the fire going and tis nice and warm," said Tom grabbing one of the bags. "Ma's expecting us all for supper. So once you're settled we'll go down to their place. Tis only five doors down."

"Awright," she said wearily. "I would like a cup of tea afore we go."

"Aye me too," said Lizzie. "And a nice warm fire sounds like just what we need. Twas so cold today in the back of that dray."

"Aye of course. Come on girls, let's go see your new house and we'll put the kettle on for your Ma and Aunt Lizzie," he said herding Susan and Esther into the house ahead of him.

.~.

Mary took the joint of beef out of the oven and set it on the bench. It smelled wonderful, and she breathed in the aroma of roasted beef with delight. After a week of nothing but mutton and potatoes she was salivating at the thought of the delicious supper, they would all have together. Tom and Jenni would be arriving soon she thought, and she was anxious to see them.

"Can I help ye Grammer?" asked Beth sidling into the kitchen sniffing the air.

"Aye ye can. Ye can finish setting the table and tell Aunt Maryann that she's needed in the kitchen." Mary opened the oven and poked the potatoes and carrots with the sharp end of a knife. They were not quite ready, but they wouldn't be much longer.

"Awright Grammer," she replied skipping off to the dining room.

Mary poured off some of the pan juices to make gravy and was just adding the flour when Maryann arrived in the kitchen.

"Ye wanted me Ma? What can I do for ye?" she queried. "Ooh, that beef smells so good." She took a small knife and carved herself off a piece. "Ooh, it tastes so good too." She licked her lips and grinned at her mother.

"Aye well seeing as you've started carving the beef, ye can finish it," said Mary admonishing at her. "The carving knife's in the second drawer I think."

Maryann found the knife and began carving the beef and putting it on the plates. "How many will there be for supper Ma?" she asked counting the plates. "I've got twelve plates here."

"Aye that sounds right," replied Mary removing the gravy from the stove.

The sound of raised voices wafted through from the parlour. "It sounds like Tom and Jenni have arrived. ye can start dishing up Maryann." Mary removed her apron and headed out of the kitchen to greet the rest of her family.

She was immediately engulfed by Susan and Esther who threw themselves at her when she entered. "Hello my darlings," she said hugging them both close.

She gave Jenni a warm hug. "Ye look exhausted," she said holding her at arm's length and looking at her. "Why don't ye set yourself down at the table, supper willna be long."

"Thank ye, Mary."

She gave Tom a quick hug before turning her attention to her youngest daughter. "Ye look so tired as well Lizzie. I know how ye feel, twas a tiring journey. Sit ye down and we'll have supper."

"I'm awright. I'll go help Maryann with supper afore I sit down," replied Lizzie.

Mary smiled at her. "Awright ye go help Maryann, I'll be there in a minute," she said before turning her attention to her final guest. "Good to see ye Henry, and thank ye for taking care of Lizzie and Jenni."

"Ye are welcome Mary," he grinned at her as his stomach gave a rather large rumble. "Supper smells good."

"Aye, well sit yourself down, it will be along in a moment," she smiled at him before heading back to the kitchen.

In no time at all supper was dished up and on the table. Richard settled himself at the head of the table and bowed his head. He gave thanks for the food they were sharing, and for their safe arrival in Wallaroo. He finished with a prayer to keep George, Alice and young Mary safe.

Mary sighed as she looked around the table at her family. She was content, and she knew she had much to be thankful for. However, she hoped and prayed that George would change his mind about Wallaroo. If she could have her eldest daughter here as well, then life would be perfect.

Chapter 10

Wallaroo 1861

Maryann and Sam's daughter arrived safely on the 17th of August. Mary realised the entire family had been nervously awaiting the birth. The memory of the son they'd lost was still fresh in everyone's mind. This had not been an easy labour for Maryann either. She'd gone into labour in the early hours of the morning and Elizabeth Jane Gilbert did not arrive until late that evening. Maryann was exhausted but elated.

She was baptised a month later with Tom and Jenni standing as her proud godparents. It was at the celebrations back at Richard and Mary's house that Sam made his big announcement.

"Firstly, I'd like to thank Richard and Mary for allowing us to stay here with them for the last few months," he said raising his glass. "We couldna have come to Wallaroo otherwise. But, now tis time I took care of my family, and so Maryann and I will be moving into our own house next week."

Everyone immediately started talking at once, offering them words of support and congratulations. "Well dunna get carried away," interrupted Sam. "Tis not our own place exactly. I've found a house to rent, but I hope that very soon we will buy our own place."

"Well tis good news," said Richard clapping him on the back. "A man needs to take care of his family and have his own place."

Over the next couple of months, life settled down into its normal rhythm. The menfolk were happy with the way things were going at the mine. They had a good pitch and were being paid well for their labours. Captain Hancock had proved to be a fair man and last survey day they'd secured their pitch for eleven shillings. Richard was a little worried that perhaps things were going too well.

Towards the end of November, Mary received welcome news from Burra. George and Alice would be coming down to visit for Christmas. She worried the trip down would be too exhausting for Alice and two-year-old Mary, but even that couldn't dampen her excitement. The thought of being surrounded by her entire family for Christmas was almost intoxicating. She spent weeks planning and baking, and couldn't have been happier on the day when the house was full to bursting.

Richard tried in vain to persuade George to make the move to Wallaroo permanently. He stubbornly refused. He agreed that the pay wasn't that great at Burra, but he truly believed the mines at Wallaroo would be short-lived.

Early in the New Year Jenni announced she was expecting again. She was blooming and thoroughly looking forward to the arrival of her fifth child. She was hoping for another son, but more than anything prayed for a healthy child. The whole time she'd been pregnant with Tommy she'd worried that something would go wrong again. The nagging doubt that something would go wrong with this baby plagued her.

In May Maryann announced she was also expecting again. She had not fully recovered her strength from having Elizabeth, and Mary thought it was too soon for her to be having another baby. Maryann had always been slim, but since Elizabeth's birth in August she'd been positively thin. She was pale with morning sickness most of the time and she looked so wan. Mary wasn't just worried for her daughter, but for her unborn bearn as well.

.~.

Jenni gave birth to a strong and healthy girl on the 12th of June 1862. She was chubby and healthy with a mop of dark hair. They named her Marianne for Tom's sister and asked Sam and Maryann to be her godparents. They agreed. They decided to wait until Maryann was over her morning sickness before having her christened.

Mary's concern for her daughter didn't subside. As soon as she got Richard and young Richard off to work she hurried down the street to Sam and Maryann's house. Her basket was laden with goodies which she hoped would give Maryann a boost. Among them was a bottle of Mr Birk's tonic water which he'd assured her would be of great benefit to any expecting mother.

Mary knocked on the door and waited. There was no answer. She was sure Maryann was home, where else would she be at this hour? She tried the doorknob. The door wasn't locked so she went inside.

"Maryann are ye there?" she called as she went into the parlour. There was no answer. She wasn't concerned, most likely she was out the back. There was no sign of nine-month-old Elizabeth, who was probably still in her crib. Mary headed out to the kitchen.

It took Mary a moment to process the scene before her. Maryann was lying on the floor in nothing but her shift. The bottom half of it was soaked in blood, and she was lying on her side with her knees pulled up around her chin.

"Maryann!" She dropped her basket and rushed to her daughter's side. "Oh my God. What's happened?" Her heart was racing as she knelt beside her. Of course, she knew what had happened; she didn't need Maryann to tell her that she'd lost her bearn.

Maryann groaned and held onto her stomach. "Oh Ma thank God you've come," she said sobbing. "I've lost my bearn."

Mary gathered her into her arms and held her close. "Oh my poor girl," she crooned and cried with her. She held her until her sobs began to subside. "Ye canna lie on this cold floor, come I'll help ye up."

She managed to get her to her feet and sat her down on a kitchen chair. "Wait here, I'll put some water on and fetch a cloth."

Maryann put her head on her arms. "Thank ye Ma," she sobbed. "Can ye check on Elizabeth as well?"

"Aye, of course." She didn't like to leave her, but she needed to get something warm to wrap her in. She hurried to the nursery first. Elizabeth was thankfully sound asleep. She went to the bedroom next and grabbed a blanket out of the box, and then rushed back to the kitchen.

"Elizabeth's still sound asleep," she said wrapping Maryann in the blanket.

She poked the fire and added another log before putting the kettle on. She then went out to the cupboard for a clean washcloth and towels. She dropped them off in the kitchen before heading out to the wash house for some rags to clean the floor with. She felt rather numb like she was going through the motions without thinking about what she was doing. She knew how hard it was to lose a child, and her heart wrenched for her daughter. It had been too soon. She'd worried about that and knew in her heart that Maryann hadn't the strength for another bearn so soon.

In no time at all she had Maryann washed and dressed in a clean shift. She tucked her into bed with the bed warmer. She knew it was going to take time for

Maryann to grieve for her loss, but she needed to make sure she was alright.

"I'm going to go and get Doctor Croft," said Mary. "I'll take Elizabeth with me so ye can rest."

Maryann shook her head. "Leave Elizabeth with me, she'll need feeding. I'll be awright till ye get back." She smiled weakly at her mother.

Mary didn't like to leave her with Elizabeth to care for but knew she was right. "Awright, but I'll fetch Lizzie to ye first. She can help ye with Elizabeth til I get back."

She went and got Elizabeth from her crib and popped her into bed with her mother. "I'll be as quick as I can." She kissed them both and hurried out the door.

.~.

Within days of losing her baby, Maryann was in the grip of a dangerously high fever. She had terrible stomach cramps and Doctor Croft was called to attend her.

Doctor Croft closed the bedroom door behind him and went to speak with Sam who was waiting in the parlour.

"Well Doctor, will she be awright?" Sam asked, his face etched with weary lines and worry.

"It's too early to say, Mr Gilbert. I've given her some laudanum for the pain," he replied soberly. "She has the childbed fever which may take a few days to break. I've treated her with a mustard plaster which should be quite beneficial." He picked up his bag. "I'll call again tomorrow. In the meantime keep a vigilant watch on her, and call me if there's any change."

Sam nodded and sank into the nearest chair.

"Thank ye, Doctor," said Mary seeing him to the door. She returned to the parlour.

"She'll be awright Sam," she said touching him on the shoulder. "Doctor Croft's taking good care of her."

"Aye I hope so," he said, though he didn't sound like he believed there was much hope.

Mary was worried for both her daughter and her son-in-law. "I'll go sit with her for a while. Why don't ye go and get some rest while ye can?"

"Awright tis probably a good idea," he said reluctantly agreeing with her.

Mary sat with her daughter for most of the afternoon. She appeared to be sleeping, and Mary was hopeful that with plenty of rest she would recover. It was late afternoon before she tiptoed out of the room to check on Sam. She found him sitting with his head in his hands in the parlour. Elizabeth was playing on a rug at his feet. He didn't look like he'd gotten any rest at all. Mary wasn't surprised, he was no doubt too worried to get any sleep. Her heart went out to him, but she couldn't think any way she could ease his worry.

"I'll go and see to supper, why don't ye go and sit with her for a while?" suggested Mary. "The doctor said we should keep a close eye on her."

He nodded and got to his feet. "Awright. Thank ye, Mary."

Mary went out to the kitchen to start preparing supper. She put Elizabeth on a rug on the floor to play while she got the vegetables ready. She was having trouble concentrating on supper she was so worried. All she could do was pray that Maryann's fever would break soon.

An anguished cry from the bedroom sent ice chills through her. Oh my God. She dropped the potato she was peeling and ran.

Sam was cradling Maryann in his arms with tears running down his face. He rocked back and forth holding her, sobbing his heart out. Mary entered the bedroom and stopped in her tracks. Fear pulsed through every fibre of her being.

"Sam?"

He sobbed and squeezed Maryann closer. "She's gone," he managed to say in-between gulps of air. "She made a horrible gasping noise and just stopped breathing."

She put her hands to her mouth to stifle her anguished cry. She felt sick, and the world seemed to tilt on its axis. Darkness engulfed her as her knees buckled beneath her and she slumped to the floor.

Chapter 11

Kooringa, July 1862

Alice collected the mail from the letterbox. She recognised her mother's writing on the creamy envelope. She was a little surprised as she'd only received a letter from her last week. She slit open the envelope and began reading the letter as she wandered up the path to the front door.

Wallaroo 24th June, 1862

Dearest Alice,

I write to you with a heavy heart and the saddest of news. Last week your dear sister Maryann miscarried the bearn she was expecting. Just a few days later she succumbed to childbed fever. We are all bereft and grief-stricken.

Our thoughts must now turn to the living that need our care. It is with this in mind that I write you. Her daughter, Elizabeth is now without a mother. Sam is beside himself with grief and is not himself. I, therefore, beseech you Alice to take on the care of your sister's child.

Jenni has her hands full with her new bearn only two weeks old. She cannot possibly take on her care for any length of time.

I am sorry to ask this of you, Alice, as I know how saddened by this news you will be. You and Maryann were always close. Please, Alice, speak with your dear husband and see if you cannot convince him that you must surely come to Wallaroo.

I hope you are all well as we are down here, and I pray that George will agree to come. Give my love and kisses to George and Mary. You, my dearest always have my love.

Your loving mother MB

Alice was stunned. She sat down on the front step and reread the letter several times. Maryann was gone. She just couldn't believe it. Of course, she would gladly do as her mother asked and take Elizabeth into her care. She almost felt a little guilty at the idea. After nearly two years of marriage, she was despairing of ever having a child with George. She had expected to have another child easily, but it hadn't happened.

The enormity of her loss suddenly overwhelmed her and she dissolved into uncontrollable sobs. She lost track of time as she sat on the doorstep and allowed her grief free rein. It was only the arrival of her dear friend Louisa that brought her to her senses.

"I see you've heard about Maryann," said Louisa sitting down on the step beside her. "I only just got word this morning myself. I canna believe it. Poor Sam, he's beside himself with grief."

Alice blew her nose and wiped the tear stains from her face, and then started crying anew. She collapsed into Louisa's arms and clung to her. "I canna believe it. My dear sweet sister. Dead."

"I know, I know," consoled Louisa as she hugged Alice to her breast. "Tis a dreadful shock for all of us."

The two women sat hugging on the step for what seemed an eternity. Eventually, the cold July day started to seep into Alice's numbed mind. "Come let's go inside," Alice finally said wiping her face on her apron. "Tis freezing out here."

Louisa gladly got to her feet. "Aye, I'm chilled to the bone."

The two women went inside and Louisa put the kettle on. After a warming cup of tea Alice was feeling much better. Her thoughts turned to George, and whether he would finally agree to move to Wallaroo.

"My mawther wants me to go to Wallaroo to take care of Elizabeth," said Alice sipping her tea. "I'm happy to do it, but I dunna know if George will go."

"Surely he will under the circumstances," said Louisa. "I would happily take Elizabeth myself, but Walter willna move to Wallaroo."

"Aye, I fear the same of George. If he willna go then I dunna know what will become of our niece."

"Surely he will go," said Louisa. "I mean your whole family is there, and there is naught here. The place will be deserted by Christmas at the rate everyone is leaving."

"Hungwy Mamma," said Mary coming into the kitchen.

"Of course ye are," said Alice immediately standing up and sweeping her daughter into her arms. "Mamma is so sorry." She kissed her and popped her on a kitchen chair. "Ye sit there and I'll get ye something to eat."

"Is that the time?" said Louisa swallowing the last of her tea. "I must be off. I'll call on ye again tomorrow Alice. I hope George agrees to go." She kissed Mary on the forehead. "Goodbye sweetheart."

It was after supper before Alice broached the subject of her niece and moving to Wallaroo with George. She knew a man with a full stomach was much more pliable than one that had just done a hard day's work with no supper. George leaned back in his chair and sighed contentedly.

"Twas a delicious supper Alice," he said. "I dunna how ye managed it with the news ye got today."

Alice smiled at him. "I'm glad ye liked it." She piled the plates on top of one another and collected the cutlery. "Of course I am devastated by the news George, but tis the living that need my care."

He nodded in agreement and reached for his pipe and tobacco.

Alice took a deep breath and steadied her nerves. "I have something to ask ye, George."

"Ah hmm, what's that my dear?"

"Well, my dear niece Elizabeth has been left without a mawther poor child. My mawther has asked if we would consider taking her into our care?"

George puffed on his pipe several times as he lit it. "Aye, well I dunna see why we couldna," he replied. "If that's what ye wish."

Alice took another deep breath. "Thank ye, George. I would like it very much." She paused as she collected her thoughts. "Tis just that it would be better if we moved to Wallaroo."

"I dunna see the need for us to move Alice," he said puffing on his pipe. "Your niece would surely come here to live?"

Alice sighed. "Well her father is in Wallaroo George. I dunna think Sam would allow us to bring her here. Twould be too far away."

"I see your point," he replied. "However, if he wants us to care for his daughter, then he'd have to allow her to come here. We live here Alice, not in Wallaroo."

"Please George, can ye not see we will need to move to Wallaroo," she said. Although she said it patiently, she was quickly losing patience with her husband. "Twould be better for all of us if we moved down there with the rest of my family. The money is better as well."

"No Alice," he said firmly crossing his arms. "I dunna think the mines will last."

Alice got to her feet and began clearing the table. "Ye are burying your head in the sand if ye think that. The mines have been up and running for nearly two years now, and they show no sign of slowing down." She didn't want to fight with George, but her emotions were raw.

She turned to face him. "I miss my family George. Ye know that I have been wanting to move to Wallaroo, and now I canna see any reason to stay here." Tears welled in her eyes and she tried to swallow the lump in her throat. "Please George I canna stand it."

She broke down and cried and was about to run from the room when George gathered her into his arms. "Hush sweetheart, I know, I know." He hugged her close and she buried her head into his shoulder.

"Please George," she sobbed and clung to him. "Please."

"Awright," he finally said. "If it means that much to ye, we'll move to Wallaroo."

Alice tried to control her sobbing and wiped the tears from her face. She looked at her husband's worried face. "Do ye mean it, George?"

"Aye. What else can I do?" he said. "I canna have my wife so unhappy. Write to your mawther and let her know we'll be there just as soon as we can arrange it."

She wrapped her arms around his neck and hugged and kissed him. "Oh thank ye. I canna tell ye what this means to me." She felt like a great weight had been lifted. She'd been so unhappy since her family had left, but until this moment hadn't realised just how miserable she'd been.

"I'll write her tonight. Thank ye."

Chapter 12

Wallaroo, August 1862

Mary hummed happily to herself as she bustled about the kitchen. Tonight she expected her entire family for supper, and it was the first time they'd all been together since Christmas. George and Alice had moved down from Burra and taken up temporary residence with Sam. It was just as well Mary thought. Sam still wasn't himself and needed someone to care for him. He'd really been neglecting himself since Maryann's death.

The only thing to mar her complete happiness was the current talk amongst the menfolk. George had brought news from Burra about a Mr Winship. He'd recently visited there to recruit miners for the Newcastle coal mines. He was on his way to Wallaroo to recruit even more miners. According to George at least fifty miners and their families were going to Newcastle from Burra. Mary worried that Tom or young Richard might be enticed to make the move as well.

Only a month later her worst fears were realised. It was after supper one evening when Tom arrived to talk with his father about Mr Winship.

"I met with the man yesterday," said Tom taking a mouthful of ale. "He's made us a very fine offer Da. He says he'll pay our fares to Newcastle and has guaranteed me wages of ten shillings a day."

Richard listened and shook his head. "Dunna be a fool, Tom. ye have your home and family here."

"What ye think tis foolish of me to want more? We have done awright here, but Da, I canna earn that kind of money from copper."

Richard drank his ale. "There's more to life than money. Family, and knowing your place in the world are far more important. Not only that, but if an offer sounds too good to be true, then it generally is." Richard was concerned for his son. He'd also heard about the generous offers being made to entice miners to Newcastle. In his mind, they sounded too good to be true.

"Well I'm not so closed-minded as that," said Tom dispassionately. "I take the man on face value. Why would he make us an offer like that if he canna deliver it?"

"I dunna know son," replied Richard. "I only know that I am worried that ye will sell up and move only to find that twas not what ye thought. Have ye discussed this with Jenni?"

Tom took a mouthful of ale and shook his head. "Not yet. I wanted to get your opinion first," he said. "To be honest with ye, I thought you'd think it a good opportunity."

"Well it might be, but tis a risk."

"Do ye not think the risk is worth the reward Da?"

Richard nodded. "Aye, but are ye sure ye want to sell your house and uproot your family?"

"Well I dunna know for sure...but I do think tis too good an offer to ignore."

"Well, I willna tell ye what to do Tom. Only ye can decide what's best for ye," said Richard draining his glass. "Your mawther and I will miss ye all very much if ye decide to go, but we willna stop ye. Just be careful Tom. Mr Winship's offer may sound better than it really is."

Tom took a deep breath and relaxed. "I thank ye Da." He got to his feet and fetched another bottle of ale from the kitchen. He came back into the parlour and poured them both another glass. He raised his, "to new ventures Da." He clinked his glass with his father's and drank.

Richard smiled at his son. "Aye, I wish ye the best of luck. Just do me one favour. Make sure ye take care of business and pay your debts afore ye leave," said Richard looking at his son seriously. "Ye will want to have a fresh start in Newcastle if that's what ye decide."

Tom grinned. He was glad to have his father on side, and a fresh start in Newcastle sounded great. "Dunna worry Da. If we decide to go I'll take care of business here first."

The two men went on talking about their current mining pitch, and had several more ales before Tom took his leave. He was feeling good. While his father hadn't exactly given him his blessing, he thought he'd taken the idea of them leaving quite well. He knew his mother would be a completely different kettle of fish. However, it wouldn't matter where he was going, or why, she wouldn't be happy about it. All in all, though, he was glad he'd planted the seed. If he had his way, they'd be going to Newcastle.

.~.

Jenni looked at him. There was no sign on his face that he was joking. No telltale curve to his mouth. "You're serious?"

"Aye," said Tom. "Mr Winship has made me a very fine offer Jenni. Ten shillings a day. I can only dream of earning that kind of money here."

"Well I agree that's a very generous wage, but Tom, do ye really want to sell up and leave?" she said astounded at the news. "I mean, we've got our own place and your family's here."

He grabbed her and took her in his arms. "Aye I know all that, but think of it, Jenni. We'd be doing it ourselves, not because my faather secured us a fair pitch. I'd be getting out from under his shadow, standing on my own two feet. Do ye see?"

She looked into his earnest dark eyes. "I didna know ye felt that way, you've never said."

"Aye well," he said letting her go. "It sounds ungrateful even to my ears. Tis not that I dunna appreciate all that my faather has done, but tis always his way. For once, I would like to secure a good position and provide for ye and the bearn's on my own."

"Ye know very well that I would follow ye to the end of the earth," she said smiling at him. "Newcastle isna that far, and if it will make ye happy then, of course, I will go with ye."

He swept her into his arms again and kissed her. "Thank ye, Jenni. I know ye dunna want to sell and move, but I swear I'll make it up to ye."

She smiled. "Well I expect ye to buy me another house at the very least," she said snuggling into him. "And I'll think of some other ways for ye to make it up to me as well."

.~.

By the end of October Tom had put their house and furniture up for sale. His agreement with Mr Winship was finalised and he was expected to be in Newcastle by the beginning of December. The steamship Wonga Wonga had been chartered by the Australian Agricultural and Coal Company to take the new recruits to Newcastle. It would be departing from the Port of Wallaroo on the 28th of November. Tom and Jenni would need to have their affairs in order and be ready to depart by then.

About a week before they were due to leave they settled the sale of their house and furniture. Tom was worried about carrying such a large sum of money with him, so he converted a good amount of it into gold. Jenni sewed most of it into the hem of Tom's jacket and her petticoat. She hoped it would be safe from any would-be thieves.

"My jacket is a little heavy, but twill be fine," said Tom taking it off and hanging it over the nearest chair. "I'll settle with the bank tomorrow and take care of Mullet's account. That will be the last of it, and we'll be free to go. I canna wait."

Jenni looked up from her sewing. "By the time we pay everyone, we willna have enough money left Tom. How much do we owe Mullet?"

"About thirty pounds I think," he replied. "I didna have enough to pay them last month, so I carried some over. Dunna worry, twill be awright."

"Thirty pounds!" Jenny did a quick calculation in her head. With what they'd got for the house and what they still had to pay the bank, she didn't think they'd have enough money to feed themselves till they got paid next. She didn't even know when that would be.

"Tom we canna afford that."

He shrugged his shoulders. "Well, we have to."

"Tom....what if we didna pay the storekeepers? What if we just left town. They would never find us."

He looked at his wife slightly aghast at her suggestion. "Jenni ye canna be serious. We must pay our debts afore we leave."

She put her sewing aside. "Think about it, Tom. We're moving to Newcastle, they willna look for us there. By the time we pay the bank I dunna think we'll have enough money. Ye are not likely to get paid until at least the end of December. What do ye suggest we live on til then?"

"We're not destitute Jenni. We have about twenty pounds. That should see us through."

"Aye, and what about another house? There is no point making this move if we go backwards. I fear we willna be able to buy another house if we pay all our debts now."

Tom rubbed his chin and mulled over her words. She was right. Money would be tight until he got paid again. He desperately wanted to buy another house as soon as they landed in Newcastle. He thought he'd have enough in gold to do that, but he had his wife and five bearns to feed.

"Ye might be right Jenni. I tell ye what. I'll pay the bank and we'll hold off paying Mullet til we get settled in Newcastle," he said pacing the floor. "Once we're set I'll send them the money we owe."

Jenni got to her feet and hugged her husband. "That's a much better idea. That way we can be sure that we'll have enough for our new house."

He hugged her close and kissed the top of her head. "Tis going to be grand Jenni."

Chapter 13

Port Clinton, 2nd December 1862

The Wonga Wonga manoeuvred into Port Clinton. It was mid-morning by the time she was secured and tied up at the one and only wharf. They would only be in port for a matter of an hour or so to take on additional supplies.

Troopers Dawson and Markham marched up the gangplank as soon as it was lowered and secure. They were met by the first mate on the main deck.

"Can I help ye gentlemen?" Considering all his passengers were miners heading for the coal mines of Newcastle, he'd not expected to be boarded by the local constabulary.

"Aye," said Dawson presenting him with the warrant. "I'm Trooper Dawson and this here is Corporal Markham. We have a warrant to arrest a Mr Thomas Bryar who we have reason to believe is on board your vessel."

"Aye," said the first mate casting his eyes over the warrant. "Well gentlemen, your warrant appears to be in order." He handed it back to Dawson. "The man leaning against the railing over there, in the grey flannel jacket, is Tom Bryar."

Dawson looked in the direction that the mate had pointed. "Thank ye." The troopers headed over to the rail where Tom was standing with his wife and children. "Mr Bryar?" enquired trooper Dawson.

Tom turned from the railing and found himself face to face with two troopers. "Aye," he replied cautiously.

"We have a warrant for your arrest Mr Bryar, and we'll be taking ye into custody," said Dawson presenting Tom with the warrant.

Tom handed Marianne to Jenni before taking the warrant and reading it. "I see," he said swallowing.

"Tom what's going on?" said Jenni alarmed at the presence of the two troopers. "There must be some mistake." She shifted Marianne onto her other hip.

"No mistake ma'am," said Dawson. "You're husband's under arrest for being an absconding debtor. This way if ye please," he said indicating that Tom should go ahead of him.

"Dunna worry Jenni, twill be awright," he said trying to calm his growing anxiety as much as Jenni's. "Where are ye taking me?"

"We'll be taking ye to Kadina where you'll face court I expect," replied Dawson. "Let's go, Bryar."

"Aye," he said. "Go back home Jenni, I'll meet ye there once I've got bail."

The troopers marched off with Tom in custody. Jenni just stared after them for a moment before her frozen mind started to work again. She hadn't seen the warrant but had a good idea who'd issued it. No doubt the Wallaroo storekeepers had discovered they'd left town.

"Why are those men taking Da?" asked Beth frowning.

Susan and Esther were equally curious, and the three of them were looking to their mother for answers. "Tis awright. We'll just go back home and we'll see your Da there."

"What about Newcassel?" asked Susan looking perplexed.

"We're not going to Newcastle yet. Maybe later," said Jenni. "Come with me." She headed across the deck to where Mr Masters the first mate was supervising the loading of supplies.

"Mr Masters," said Jenni breathing heavily as she came to his side. "I'll be needing my sea chest and trunk. I'll be returning to Wallaroo."

"Aye I expected as much," he said looking her up and down. "I'll have them unloaded for ye."

"Thank ye, Mr Masters," she replied haughtily. "I'll just gather my other belongings then."

"Very well," said Masters going back to his work.

"Beth, stay here while I go get our portmanteau. Hold onto Tommy's hand and dunna let him go anywhere."

"Aye Mamma," she replied taking hold of her young brother.

Jenni hurried down below. She put Marianne in one of the hammocks while she quickly stuffed the loose clothing and their other items into the portmanteau. Tom mentioned getting bail. Well, he obviously didn't think he'd be in gaol for any length of time then. She took a deep breath and scooped Marianne into her arms. God, how had this happened? She hurried back up to the main deck where the rest of the children were waiting.

"Awright Beth take Tommy by the hand and hang onto him," said Jenni as she headed for the gangplank. "Dunna let him fall for God's sake."

Jenni waited on the wharf with her children while her trunks were unloaded. Thankfully it wasn't a hot day. There was no cover whatsoever and she prayed they wouldn't have to wait long. Two-year-old Tommy was interested in all the comings and goings and was beginning to get restless. She'd only been waiting about twenty minutes when she noticed her trunks being carried down the gangplank.

"Stay here," she said to the children before heading over to the gangway.

"I'll be needing some assistance to get my trunks to Wallaroo," she said to the first sailor. "Would ye be able to help me?"

He looked at her. "Sorry missus, we're to unload 'em and that's all. We'll be settin' sail just as soon as it's done." He brushed passed her. "We'll put 'em over there," he said to his companion. They headed across to the other side of the wharf where they dropped her trunk and chest.

Jenni followed them. "Please I dunna know what to do." She was desperate and could feel the panic rising in her. How was she supposed to get herself and their luggage back home? She hoisted Marianne onto her hip. "Surely ye can help me."

The sailor looked at her and sighed. "I'm not from these parts. Sorry missus I can't help ye." He and his companion turned and headed back to the ship.

Jenni felt panic grip her. She sat down on the trunk and dissolved into tears.

She couldn't believe the predicament she was in and she needed Tom. Finally, she took several deep breaths and pulled herself together. Tom was relying on her to get herself and the bearns back home. She'd have to find a way.

She noticed there were several men with carts who'd delivered the supplies that were loaded onto the Wonga Wonga. She wiped the tears from her face and walked over to them.

"Excuse me. Would ye be able to take my trunks to Wallaroo?" she asked the first man she came to.

He was just about to climb up onto his dray when she spoke to him. He looked her up and down, slightly surprised by the look on his face.

"Ma'am," he said doffing his hat at her. "I'm not going that way, sorry." He climbed up onto his dray and was about to click his horses into action when she put her hand on his leg to stop him.

"Please, I dunna know what to do. I have to get myself and my luggage to Wallaroo."

He groaned. "Look ma'am I only do deliveries and such in Port Clinton."

"Well could ye at least take me and my trunks to some lodgings?" she said desperate to get someone to help her. "I can pay ye, and I can get a conveyance from there."

"Awright ma'am," he said climbing down from his dray. "Where's your trunks then?"

"Oh thank ye. I canna tell ye how much I appreciate your help. This way, they're just on the wharf," she said pointing to her trunk and chest. "I'll just go fetch my bearns."

Chapter 14

Kadina, 10ᵗʰ December 1862

Tom looked outwardly calm as he stood in the dock and waited for the charges to be read. He was confident the matter could be settled, but he was beside himself with worry for Jenni. He'd abandoned her in Port Clinton a week ago and had received no word. All he could do was hope and pray that she'd somehow managed to get herself and bearns safely to Wallaroo.

He shifted his weight as he waited for the Magistrate to arrive. James Mullet and Henry Graham were seated with their lawyer talking quietly. He sighed.

The clerk of courts finally came through the imposing wooden door. "All rise. Mr James Shepherdson presiding."

The Magistrate came into the court and sat down behind the bench. Tom thought he looked like a fair man. He was in his mid-fifties and looked alert and intelligent.

"Mr Thomas Bryar is brought before this court on charges of being an absconded debtor," said the clerk. "The plaintiff's, in this case, are Mr James Mullet and Mr Henry Graham, storekeepers of Wallaroo." He handed several papers to the Magistrate before sitting down.

"Your honour. My clients claim is for the amount of forty-seven pounds eleven shillings and threepence, for goods delivered."

Mr Shepherdson nodded. "How do you plead Mr Bryar?"

"Your honour, I am only indebted for thirty-two pounds fourteen shillings and twopence," said Tom.

"Mr Robson please present your evidence in support of your client's claim."

Mr Robson shuffled through several pages before him and then spoke to his clients. They spoke so quietly that Tom couldn't hear what was being said.

"Your honour I request an adjournment so that the evidence can be gathered."

"Very well, we will adjourn until nine o'clock tomorrow morning."

Tom had no intention of spending another night in custody. He had to find Jenni and the bearns. "Your honour. I would like to give bail so that I may see to my wife and family."

Mr Shepherdson nodded and then addressed Mr Robson. "Do you have any objections to bail being posted for Mr Bryar?"

He quickly conferred with his clients. "None sir."

"Very well. Bail is posted with a surety of twenty pounds Mr Bryar. You will appear before this court again tomorrow morning. Case adjourned."

"Thank ye, your honour."

.~.

Tom left the court and walked to his father's house. He hoped they would have news of Jenni. It was mid-afternoon before he arrived and he knocked on the door.

"Oh tis ye," said his mother when she answered the door. "I canna believe that ye would have the nerve to present yourself at our door."

It wasn't the greeting he'd expected. "Hello, Ma. Have ye seen Jenni?"

"Aye more's the pity," she replied scowling at him.

"Ma I dunna know what you've heard, but I was forced to abandon Jenni and the bearns at Port Clinton. I've been worried sick about them."

"How do ye think we feel? I was down at the store buying supplies and talking to Henry Graham. I tells him that ye got a fine offer from Mr Winship and that you've gone to Newcastle. And what do ye think he says to me?" she said disdainfully. "He canna have done that Mrs Bryar, he's hasn't paid his account. Ye have shamed us something dreadful."

"Ma it wasna like that. I fully intended to pay him, but Jenni was worried about us not having enough money. She suggested we pay once we were settled in Newcastle."

"So twas your wife's advice ye took over your faather's?" she said still scowling at him. "Ye should've paid them. As for your wife, you'll find her back at your old place."

"Thank ye Ma," he said with a sigh of relief. "Ye have to believe me though, I never intended to shame ye or faather."

"Well, ye have done." She shut the door and left him standing on the doorstep.

He took several deep breaths. There would be time aplenty later to set his mother straight. He had to see Jenni first. He headed down the street to his old house. He wasn't entirely sure whether his mother was serious that Jenni was at their old house, so he knocked on the door.

"Tom," exclaimed Jenni when she opened it. She wrapped her arms about his neck and kissed him. "I canna believe tis ye. I've been worried sick and I didna know what to do."

"Oh Jenni," he held her in his arms and breathed in her familiar scent. "I've been worried sick about ye and the bearns ever since I left ye in Port Clinton. I'm ever so sorry Jenni."

Jenni clung to him and sobbed. "I was so scared," she wept. "I didna know what to do."

"Hush tis awright," said Tom holding her close. "Let's go inside and ye can tell me how ye come to be here."

They went inside the house and Jenni explained how she'd managed to get a conveyance back to Wallaroo. "Once I got back here though I had nowhere to go. I knew your Ma and Da wouldna have room for us, so I went to see John Hoskins who we'd sold the house to," she said wiping her tears away with the back of her hand. "Anyways, I told him how we'd had to come back and asked him if I could stay in our old house. He told me he'd be renting it out once he'd cleaned it up, so I asked him to rent it to me right away. Thank God he agreed, else I dunna know where we'd have gone."

"You've rented our old house back?"

"Aye. I didna know what else to do Tom. I didna know how long you'd be in gaol, and so aye I've rented the house back. I had to have somewhere for me and the bearns."

"Of course," he said hugging her. "Tis a fine idea, at least until we can get passage booked for Newcastle."

"So what happened with Mullet and Graham? Is it sorted out then?"

"Aye. I've posted bail and I have to go back to court tomorrow. I expect the matter will be settled and then we'll be free to go."

"Oh thank God for that. I swear I'll never suggest anything like that again. It's been a nightmare."

.~.

Tom returned to the Kadina Court the following morning. He hoped the matter would be dealt with today. He was anxious to arrange passage to Newcastle as soon as possible. Now that he'd missed the chartered ship he'd have to find a coastal vessel going to Newcastle himself. Further delays could mean that he would miss out on the job offer made to him by Mr

Winship. His apprehension was growing as he waited to be called.

It was just after nine o'clock when the clerk of courts opened the door and stepped out. "All persons for the matter of Mullet and Graham versus Bryar," he called before disappearing back into the courtroom.

Tom got to his feet and followed Mullet and Graham and their lawyer into the court. They took their seats at one of the tables and Tom sat down at the other. He hoped they wouldn't have to wait long for the Magistrate to arrive.

"All rise, Mr James Shepherdson presiding," said the clerk of courts as the large wooden door opened.

The Magistrate came in and settled himself behind the bench.

The clerk handed several pages to Mr Shepherdson. "These are the particulars of the adjourned case of Mullet and Graham versus Bryar. The plaintiffs are represented by Mr Robson." He sat down again.

"Have you had sufficient time to gather your evidence to support the claims of your clients Mr Robson?"

"Yes your Honor," he replied. "If I may present these accounts, your Honor. They list the amounts owed to my clients by Mr Bryar."

The clerk took the pages and handed them to the Magistrate, who quickly read through them. "The amount claimed is still forty-seven pounds eleven shillings and threepence," he said looking up. "Which amounts to you dispute Mr Bryar?"

Over the next couple of hours, every item listed was examined in detail. Tom disputed several items and after going back and forth they finally came to an agreed amount.

"The amount agreed upon then is forty-three pounds nine shillings and sixpence," said the Magistrate. "I find in favour of the plaintiffs in this case, and Mr Bryar shall also cover their costs."

"Your Honor, I request to be allowed time in order to pay," said Tom.

"Do you have any objection Mr Robson," asked the Magistrate.

"Yes, your Honor. Mr Bryar has recently sold his property in Wallaroo for the amount of one hundred and thirty pounds," said Mr Robson. "I also believe that he applied to the local bank to exchange his notes for gold. Under such circumstances, he should be required to pay immediately."

"Agreed Mr Robson," said Mr Shepherdson. "Mr Bryar you are hereby ordered to pay the amount of judgement at once or be imprisoned for forty days."

Tom swallowed. Forty days gaol was out of the question. "Your Honor, I can pay twenty pounds in cash now. I also offer security for the balance to be paid by Monday."

"Will your clients accept the defendant's settlement Mr Robson?"

Mr Robson consulted with Mullet and Graham. They talked together in hushed voices and Tom prayed they'd agree. He waited patiently.

"Yes, your Honor. My clients will accept the settlement."

"Very well. You are released from custody Mr Bryar and dismissed."

"Thank ye, your Honor," said Tom standing as the Magistrate left the courtroom. He breathed a massive sigh of relief.

After paying the storekeepers the agreed twenty pounds he left the court. It was late afternoon before he arrived home and gave Jenni the good news.

"Thank God that is over," said Jenni hugging him. "So we have no money til Monday then?"

"Aye. I have a few shillings tis all. Dunna worry. On Monday I'll change enough of the gold back into notes to pay

Mullet and Graham, and some for us as well," replied Tom pouring himself an ale. "Then we'll see if we can book passage for Newcastle. I am worried that it may already be too late."

Chapter 15

Wallaroo, 15th December 1862

Tom spent the morning taking care of business. He changed some of their gold back into notes and paid the final amount owing to Mullet and Graham. He then made enquiries at the Port of Wallaroo for any vessels they were expecting that might be sailing for Newcastle. He had no luck. The best he could find was a ship bound for Sydney which was due in the following week.

He intended to discuss their options with Jenni that evening over supper. However, when he returned home he found Jenni in a state.

"What's amiss Jenni?"

"Tis your Ma and Da," she replied wiping the tears from her eyes. "They've been spreading rumours about me all over town."

Tom wasn't entirely surprised considering the reception he'd received from his mother last Thursday. He gathered her in his arms and hugged her. "Dunna worry, I'll speak with my Da about it."

She clung to him and sobbed. "Tis so unfair what they're saying. I willna be able to show my face."

"It canna be that bad Jenni," he soothed. "What is it they're saying?"

She wiped her eyes and looked at him. "They say tis all my fault ye were arrested and that I've disgraced the family. I hear say that I'm wicked." She dissolved into more tears.

It was too much. After the ordeal, they'd been through, and poor Jenni being stranded in Port Clinton, she didn't deserve this treatment from his family. He was furious that they'd blackened her name around town.

He held her until her sobs subsided. "Dunna listen to them, ye know tis not true," he said. "I'll go and set my family straight after supper. I promise ye they'll stop their slandering."

After supper, he walked down to his parent's house. He was feeling nervous as he opened the front door and went inside, but he was determined to confront his father. Dick Vivien, a friend of young Richards was sitting in the parlour and looked up when he entered.

"Evening Tom," he greeted him.

"What have ye to say about my wife?" said Tom as he went to go through to the kitchen.

"Nothing," replied Dick staring at him with raised eyebrows.

Tom went into the kitchen and saw his father standing by the table. Richard looked up at him as he entered.

"What about you old man?" said Tom approaching him. "What have ye got to say about my wife?"

Richard sneered at him and raised his hand to hit him. Tom stepped aside and then struck his father square in the jaw. He staggered backwards rubbing his chin where Tom had landed the blow.

"Don't ye come in here after the way ye have shamed us all. Get out!"

"I dunna give a shit, I'll take your bloody head off," said Tom raising his arm to defend himself as his father went to strike him again. He managed to grab hold of Richard by the collar.

Young Richard came hurrying into the kitchen. "Let go of faather," he said as he tried to hit Tom and separate them.

Tom grabbed his young brother with his other hand, but he managed to twist out of his grasp. "Stay out of this, tis between me and Da."

"I'll kill ye if ye dunna let him go," said young Richard picking up the axe which was leaning against the hearth.

Tom was distracted by the axe in his brother's hand and his father wrestled himself free. He grabbed hold of Tom around the waist and shoved him as hard into the kitchen table. Tom landed on his back on the table with his father on top of him. A box of specimen rocks broke and scattered.

Lizzie having heard the commotion came running into the kitchen as well. She called to her mother, "they're going to kill Da." She grabbed hold of Tom's hair and began pulling. "Leave faather alone," she screamed and hit him.

Tom struggled to free himself from his father's grip, but he had his whole weight on him. He didn't see young Richard lift the axe over his head. He only felt the weight of it when it sliced into his shoulder and he felt his collar bone crunch under the impact. He couldn't be sure where the next blow came from either, only that he was knocked senseless.

The three of them continued to hit and beat on Tom for several minutes. Finally, Richard grabbed him by the hair and dragged him from the kitchen, through the parlour and out the front door. He was still intent on beating him to a pulp until a passerby intervened.

"Get off him," said John Oates pushing Richard aside.

Tom was bleeding profusely. His right arm was hanging uselessly by his side as he started to stagger towards his house. He only managed to go about thirty yards before he fell down unconscious in the dirt. John Oates called to another man, John Symonds to help him.

"Do ye know him?" asked John Oates as he lifted Tom to his feet.

"Aye," replied Symonds. "Tis Tom Bryar, he lives just a few doors down." They each got on either side of him and carried him to his house.

Jenni opened the door and gasped. Two men, one she recognised as John Symonds were supporting Tom between them. His shirt was soaked with blood and he was still bleeding from a four-inch wound along his collar bone.

"Oh my God.....come in," she said. "Bring him in here." She led the men into the bedroom where they laid Tom out on the bed.

She knelt beside the bed and examined the wound. "Twill need stitching. What happened?"

"His faather was beating him when I come across them outside the house," said John Oates looking ashen-faced. "Shall I fetch Dr Croft for ye?"

"Aye. Thank ye."

Oates immediately headed out of the room. Jenni covered Tom with a coverlet. "Thank ye for bringing him home, John. I canna believe his faather would do this to him."

The shock of seeing him was beginning to wear off, and she was on the verge of tears. It was all her fault. If only she hadn't suggested they pay the storekeepers later. "The doctor will no doubt need hot water and towels. I'll go see to it. Would ye stay here with him?"

"Aye, of course," he replied sitting down on the blanket box. "Jenni, I'm ever so sorry we didna get there earlier."

"Dunna be sorry. I canna thank ye enough for bringing him home." She went out to the kitchen and stoked the fire and put the kettle on. She gathered clean towels and took a few deep breaths to steady her nerves. She was glad the children were all abed, and Marianne should sleep til the morning.

A knock on the front door startled her, and she hurried to open it.

"Doctor Croft thank ye for coming. He's in here," she said leading the doctor through to the bedroom.

Doctor Croft put his bag down and approached Tom. He examined the wound. "Can you hear me, Mr Bryar?"

Tom groaned and turned his head towards the doctor. "Aye."

"Good," he said. "Mrs Bryar if you could bring some clean towels, some hot water and a washcloth please. I'll need to clean your husband's wound."

"Aye of course." She hurried off to the kitchen to gather the towels and water for the doctor.

She returned with the items just as the Doctor was cutting Tom out of his shirt. Jenni could see a four-inch gash along Tom's collar bone which was oozing blood. She gasped. My God was that bone she could see? Doctor Croft poured a draft of laudanum and gave it to Tom.

"It will help to numb the pain while I clean the wound," he said. He then proceeded to clean away most of the blood before prodding the wound with a pair of forceps. He removed a fragment of bone. "It's a clean-cut Mr Bryar. However, the bone's splintered and some sloughing may occur."

Tom groaned. "Will my arm be any good?"

"I don't believe it'll be a permanent injury," he said as he began stitching the wound together.

Tom winced with each stitch that pulled the skin together but otherwise remained still. Doctor Croft applied a clean gauze to the wound and bandaged around Tom's upper torso. "The dressing will need changing daily," he said as he fastened it. "It will also be better if you can keep that arm as immobile as possible."

Tom nodded. "Thank ye, Doctor."

Doctor Croft put his instruments back in his bag and handed a small vial to Jenni. "I'll come by and check on you tomorrow. If the pain gets too bad give him another draft of laudanum," said Doctor Croft. "In the meantime, I recommend bed rest."

"Thank ye," said Jenni.

It was after midnight before Jenni had seen the doctor, John Oates and John Symonds out. She closed the front door and leaned against it for a moment. She felt emotionally drained and exhausted. She wondered if Tom would report the incident to the police. Her mind was having trouble accepting the fact that his father had done this. She was horrified at the thought.

131

Tom was not well enough the next day to speak to anyone, let alone the police. He was still in bed resting when his sister Alice arrived late in the afternoon. Jenni greeted her, unsure where her allegiance lay.

She gave Jenni a warm hug which allayed her fears somewhat. "I canna believe what has happened," said Alice with a worried expression on her face. "I heard that Tom and Da had a massive argument and that Tom was injured. How is he?"

"Not good," replied Jenni. "He has a ghastly wound on his shoulder which has cut him to the bone."

Alice put her hand over her mouth and sucked in her breath. She was clearly shocked by the news. "I hear it was an accident. Ma told me that Tom fell onto the table and was cut by a knife lying there," she said.

Jenni shook her head. "To be honest with ye Alice I dunna know what happened exactly," said Jenni. "Tom hasn't been in any condition to tell me the details. But, I am not so sure it was an accident."

"Well ye know I love my faather and my brother both. Regardless of what happened between them, I willna take sides."

"I thank ye for that Alice. I think the rest of the family are well against us," said

Jenni sighing. "I know your Ma blames me for all of this."

"Aye I think she does," said Alice nodding her head in agreement. "Dunna worry about that Jenni. Ye need to take care of Tom and your family. I'll come by again tomorrow when Tom's feeling more up to receiving visitors if that's awright?"

"Aye, that'll be fine. I'll tell him ye called, I know he'll be glad that ye did," said Jenni hugging her.

Alice left and Jenni realised that she was feeling a lot better. It was comforting to know that at least one member of the family wasn't against them.

Chapter 16

Wallaroo, 17th December 1862

After spending two days in bed, Tom was feeling stiff and sore. His shoulder was painful, and every time he moved it felt like the stitches were being pulled. Jenni finished securing the sling Doctor Croft had left for him.

"Thank ye, Jenni," he said smiling at her. It felt much better to have his right arm in the sling. Apart from removing the useless feeling of having his arm dangling down, his shoulder was much less painful.

"You're welcome. Are ye sure ye want to do this?"

"Aye I'm sure," he replied grim-faced. "I canna believe my Da did this, but I'll be damned if I'll allow him to get away with it. I want him charged." He settled himself back in bed against the pillows and Jenni pulled the coverlet up over him.

"Awright then. If ye are ready I'll send in Corporal Bentley."

Corporal Bentley was ensconced with Tom for nearly an hour. Jenni worried that Tom would be exhausted by the time he'd given his statement. She paced the kitchen until she finally heard the bedroom door open. She hurried into the hall just in time to see the Corporal emerging.

"I'll take care of the matter from here Mr Bryar," he was saying as he came out of the bedroom. He noticed Jenni standing in the hall. "Thank ye, Mrs Bryar. I think I've got everything I need."

"Ye are welcome Corporal."

She saw the Corporal to the door and wished him well, before going to check on Tom. He was lying back with his eyes closed. She wasn't sure if he was already asleep or not but tiptoed out of the room.

.~.

Richard was not surprised to see Corporal Bentley and Trooper Doyle on his doorstep. He'd been expecting a visit from the constabulary since Monday night.

"Come in Corporal," said Richard leading the two men into the parlour. "How can I help ye?"

"I think ye have a good idea why we're here Mr Bryar," said Corporal Bentley. "We've just come from your son's house, where he's lying abed having been lamed. He's accused ye of assaulting him with an axe."

"Aye, well I'm very sorry for whats happened Corporal, but I can assure ye I didna attack my son with an axe."

"That's all very well," said the Corporal. "However, we require ye to accompany us. We are placing ye under arrest for felonious assault. The Magistrate can decide if ye are guilty or no."

Trooper Doyle had been poking around the house and emerged from the kitchen carrying an American axe. "Is this the axe in question?" he asked Richard.

"I dunna know," he replied. "If ye are asking if that's my axe, then aye it is. Tis the only one I own."

"Well we'll be taking that as evidence," said Corporal Bentley. "After ye Mr Bryar."

Mary came through from the kitchen wiping her hands on her apron. "What's going on Richard?" she said looking at the two Corporals.

"Twould appear I'm under arrest Mary. Dunna worry I've done naught wrong," he said as he preceded the two Corporals out the door.

Mary hurried after them with panic clear on her face. "Ye canna arrest my husband. Please I dunna know what my son has accused him of, but tis a family matter."

"It is a matter for the law now Mrs Bryar," said Corporal Bentley putting on his hat.

"Dunna worry Mary," Richard called over his shoulder as they started down the street. "I'll be home afore supper."

Richard was brought before the Magistrate that very afternoon. Doctor Croft was called to give evidence, and on application from Corporal Bentley, he was remanded in custody for a week.

.~.

24th December, 1862

Jenni opened the door and was surprised to see Corporal Bentley. "Afternoon Corporal, won't ye come in," she said standing back to allow him to enter.

Tom was sitting in the parlour with Marianne playing on the floor at his feet. He looked up as the Corporal came in. "Corporal Bentley," said Tom equally surprised to see him.

"I'm sorry to come by on Christmas Eve like this," he said apologetically as he removed his hat.

"Not at all," said Jenni. "I was just making a pot of tea, would ye like a cup?"

"No, thank ye, Mrs Bryar. I've just come by to speak with ye about your father."

"Well at least have a seat Corporal," said Tom gesturing to the chair opposite him by the window.

Jenni went off to the kitchen leaving the Corporal to speak with Tom.

"Who's that Mamma?" enquired Susan peeking into the parlour.

"Tis Corporal Bentley, he's come to talk to your faather," replied Jenni wringing her hands together. "Run outside and play with Beth and Esther. And keep an eye on Tommy for me as well."

"Awright Mamma," she said skipping off.

Jenni prepared a pot of tea and set three cups on the tray along with a jug of milk. Although Constable Bentley had declined her offer of tea, she thought it would look a bit rude if she only took two cups out. She picked up the tray and went back into the parlour.

"Anyways, after further enquiry we couldn't find any evidence against him," said Corporal Bentley. "He was released from custody this morning. I thought ye ought to know."

"What's this?" said Jenni placing the tray down on the side table.

"The Corporal was just saying they've released Da," replied Tom. "Apparently, he didna do it."

Jenni looked stunned. "Well if your faather didna attack ye, who did?" She poured a cup of tea and handed it to Tom. "Are ye sure ye wouldna like a cup Corporal?"

"Quite sure thank ye," he replied. "Over the past week, we have spoken with all those that were at your father's house that evening. Based on the evidence of John Symonds, we have arrested your younger brother Richard. He's been committed for trial."

Tom was halfway through swallowing a mouthful of tea. He coughed. "What! Young Richard?"

"Aye," replied Corporal Bentley. "The evidence against him is without a doubt. Mr Symonds has also stated that your brother intended ye more harm. He told him that it was not half bad enough and that he wished he'd cut your head off. I am sorry Mr Bryar, I can see that it's come as a shock to ye."

"Aye, it has," replied Tom as he tried to comprehend the news. His memories from that night were foggy and disjointed.

He remembered young Richard being there. He had hold of him at one point and he thought he'd kicked him in the shins. He had a vague memory of young Richard threatening him if he didn't let go of his father. He didn't remember much else about him.

Jenni wasn't so shocked by the news. She sipped her tea and remained quiet, however. She would tell Tom about young Richard's behaviour last year while he was away in Wallaroo after the Corporal had left.

"The trial will be held at Kadina in the New Year. It'll take several weeks for the Prosecutor to issue summons to the witnesses," said the Corporal. "Ye will be advised well ahead of time."

"Well I thank ye for coming to tell us this personally," said Tom. "I still canna believe twas my young brother."

"Aye. Well I wish ye both a happy Christmas," said Corporal Bentley getting to his feet.

"Thank ye, Corporal Bentley," said Jenni rising and seeing him to the door. "I hope ye and your family have a happy Christmas as well." Jenni closed the door and leaned against it for a moment.

"I canna believe young Richard did this," said Tom sipping his tea. "I doesna make sense to me. We've never even had an argument."

"Well, while ye were away with your faather and Sam, and I was staying with Alice in Burra, your brother made his feelings about us very clear," said Jenni sitting down. "He was very resentful of you being down here with your faather and him being left behind. He was so jealous of ye Tom, he said your faather favoured ye."

Tom stared at her. "What? Why did ye not tell me?"

"I didna think it was important at the time," replied Jenni. "Anyway, I thought once he came to Wallaroo he'd get over his jealousy. He seemed to."

Tom nodded. "Aye, he's been fine. What a fool though. The argument was between me and my Da. There was no need for anyone else to interfere. He'll likely go to gaol for it."

"Hmm, your mawther must be beside herself," said Jenni draining her cup. "Do ye think I should go see her?"

"No," said Tom shaking his head. "She willna take kindly to ye Jenni. Tis best to wait and see if she comes to us."

"Do ye think she will?"

"I dunna know. But, I dunna want ye going anywhere near my family until this matter's settled," he said. "Tis best to wait and see what they do."

Chapter 17

Wallaroo, 25ᵗʰ December 1862

Jenni could not remember having such a miserable Christmas in her life. The Christmas after her father had died had been a sad affair, particularly for her mother. This year though was depressing for a lot of different reasons.

Tom of course still had his arm in a sling and wasn't much help with carving the goose. He did his best to entertain the bearns, but they were full of questions that couldn't be answered. It wasn't likely they would be seeing either Grammer or Granfer today. Jenni had hoped her mother-in-law might have come to see them on Christmas Eve, but she knew in her heart that she blamed her for this whole affair. She didn't come.

So she only had her own little family to serve dinner for. At least Alice and George and the girls would be coming for supper. She was glad they at least had not deserted them. She knew it was still too soon to hope that Tom and his father would make peace. She prayed they would soon.

Tom was so worried that he would never work again, and she knew he missed his father's counsel. Whenever she caught him unawares, he just looked so lost and sad. She didn't know what to do to help him.

Alice and George arrived for supper armed with gifts for the bearns, and words of support for Tom. Alice announced she was expecting again. Jenni knew she'd almost given up hope after more than two years of marriage.

"Congratulations to ye both," said Tom raising his glass awkwardly with his left hand. "Tis wonderful news and God knows we could do with some."

"Thank ye," smiled Alice. "I know, it's been an awful time for all of us. Ma and Da will come around though, I just know it."

Tom tried to hide the grimace. "Ye have always thought the best of people Alice. I do hope ye are right, but I dunna think twill happen any day soon. Not with young Richard's trial still ahead of us."

"Your mawther must be so upset at young Richard's arrest," said Jenni as she piled the dirty plates on top of one another. "I canna imagine how I would feel if it was one of my bearns."

"Aye, she's beside herself over it," said Alice getting to her feet to help Jenni.

"The thing is he's so young and he's likely going to go to gaol for it."

"Twill not be good for him to go to gaol," said George shaking his head. "I mean he's only just fifteen, isn't he? Got his whole life ahead of him."

"Aye," said Tom. "I dunna want to think about it."

"What about ye Tom?" said George sipping his cider. "Is your shoulder mending?"

"Aye, at least Dr Croft seems to think so. I still canna move my arm from the shoulder, and he doesna know if it will come back or not," said Tom. "I dunna know if I will ever be able to go back down the mines. I'm just so afeard I may never work again. I've a wife and five bearns and I canna see what I'm to do."

George looked at him sympathetically, but Tom knew he had no idea how he was feeling. "Give it time Tom. I'm sure twill get better aye."

"Oh aye I'm sure ye are right," said Tom hoping that George would drop the subject. Jenni and Alice were in the kitchen washing dishes and Tom suggested they retire to the parlour where they wouldn't be overheard. "How's my Da George? I mean, how is he really?"

"Well, of course, he's very sorry for what's happened, and I think he thinks that if ye and Richard could just make up twould all go away."

Tom nodded. He could well imagine his father thinking that. In his mind, it should simply be a matter of him making peace with his brother. Perhaps if young Richard hadn't wished him more harm he could forgive him. He certainly had no forgiveness in his heart yet.

"Aye, faather has always thought things could be easily fixed," said Tom. "Tis out of my hands though. The law will take its course now."

.~.

The date for the trial was set for the 12th of February, 1863. Corporal Bentley delivered a summons for Tom to appear. He felt ill at the very thought of giving evidence against his brother.

"Now, remember if we are not here when ye get home from school, ye are to go to Aunt Alice's," said Jenni kissing Esther on the forehead. "She'll be expecting ye."

"Why canna we go to Grammer's?" asked Susan picking up her satchel.

"She willna be home. Now have a good day at school and dunna forget ye are to go to Aunt Alice."

"We won't forget Mamma," said Beth as she headed for the front door followed by her two young sisters.

Jenni heaved a sigh of relief as she watched them walk down the street. She'd expected more questions than that and suspected that Beth knew what was going on. No doubt they'd been eavesdropping.

She slung the bag of extra clothes and clouts over one shoulder and eight-month-old Marianne over the other. "Are ye right to go then?" she said to Tom who had Tommy by the hand.

"Aye."

It was only a short walk to Alice and George's house. Tommy chatted all the way which meant Tom didn't have a chance to dwell on the impending trial. He was such a curious little boy and found wonder in everything. They left their two youngest children in Alice's care.

"I've told the girls to come to ye if we are not home when they get out of school," said Jenni kissing Marianne on the cheek. "I hope these two willna be too much trouble."

"They'll be fine," said Alice taking Marianne in her arms. "Go, ye dunna want to be late."

"Thank ye for taking care of the bearns Alice," said Tom. "Tis a great relief for me to have Jenni by my side today."

"Ye are welcome. Dunna worry they'll be fine with me."

Chapter 18

Kadina, February 1863

Tom and Jenni arrived at the Court with time to spare and went inside. Richard, Mary and Lizzie were already there along with several others including Dick Vivien. It was the first time Tom had seen his father since that fateful night. He thought he looked fine. He appeared to be his usual calm and relaxed self. His mother on the other hand looked positively petrified. He sucked in several deep breaths as he tried to calm his nerves. He knew his anxiety would be sky high before he was even called to the witness stand.

The Clerk of Courts approached them with a bible under one arm and several documents in the other. "What's your name, sir?"

"Tom Bryar," he replied standing up.

The Clerk looked down the page in his hand. "Very good. I'll need you to swear on the Bible please," he said handing it to Tom. "Do you swear to tell the truth, and nothing but the truth so help you, God."

"I do," he replied.

"Thank you."

He took the bible from Tom and approached the next person who had just arrived. It was John Symonds. Tom knew John was here to testify against his brother, and he felt ill in the pit of his stomach. He was feeling so anxious and just wanted today to be over. Jenni slipped her hand into his and squeezed. He sighed and took several deep breaths. It would be alright - he had Jenni by his side.

The door opened and the jury of twelve men walked in and took their places. Two troopers appeared through another door accompanied by young Richard. Tom sucked in a breath. His brother looked so young and scared. He'd been in custody for nearly two months and Tom thought he was looking thin and gaunt.

A few minutes later the Clerk of Courts stood up and addressed the court. "All stand for His Honor Justice Gwynne."

The Magistrate entered the court and took his seat at the bench. "This is the matter of Richard Bryar charged with felonious assault upon his brother. All parties have been sworn in," said the Clerk as he handed several documents to Justice Gwynne. "Mr Ingleby is representing the defendant and Mr George Hamilton for the Crown." He then sat back down.

"Mr Hamilton please call your first witness," said the Magistrate.

"Thank you, Your Honor," said Mr Hamilton getting to his feet. "I call the prosecutor in this case, Mr Thomas Bryar."

Tom's stomach did a backflip when his name was called. He sucked in a deep breath and got to his feet. He felt like all the eyes in the room were on him as he crossed the floor to the witness stand.

"Mr Bryar would you please tell the court what you recollect from the evening of the fifteenth of December last. I believe you went to your father's house between the hours of seven and eight pm?"

"Aye, that's right," replied Tom nervously licking his lips. "My faather was in the kitchen, and I said to him what a shame it was the way he and my mawther were abusing my wife. My faather raised his hand to strike me. I defended myself and grabbed him by the collar. Several others then rushed into the room."

"When you first saw your father, was he standing near the fire shaving down a piece of wood?"

"He had something in his hands, but I canna say what it was for sure," said Tom.

"Go on Mr Bryar. Then what happened?"

"Well I had hold of my faather with my left hand, and my brother Richard came in. I took hold of him with my right hand," said Tom. "Young Richard slipped from my grasp and picked up the axe, and said I'll bloody kill ye."

"Had you had any previous quarrel with your brother Mr Bryar?"

"No," replied Tom.

"What happened after your brother escaped your grasp?"

"He took hold of the axe with both hands and struck me on the shoulder with it. I fell to the ground and was bleeding badly. Someone else started to beat on me. I'm not sure what happened after that, I was knocked senseless. The next thing I recall is that I was lying on the road outside the house." He took several deep breaths and tried to calm his nerves. It helped if he just looked straight ahead and not at his mother and father who were sitting in the front row.

"Initially you did not say that your brother attacked you with an axe. Why was that?"

He took a deep breath and focused on Mr Hamilton. "I wasna very well when I gave my statement to Corporal Bentley. My memory wasna clear and I was confused."

"Thank you, Mr Bryar you may step down," said Mr Hamilton as he shuffled through several papers.

Tom returned to his seat beside Jenni and took her hand in his. He was so relieved that his part in the proceedings was over, and hoped to God that Mr Ingleby wouldn't want to question him as well.

"I call Mr John Symonds to the stand," said Mr Hamilton.

John Symonds walked confidently across the court to the witness stand.

"Mr Symonds. Would you please tell the court what you recall from the evening in question?"

"Aye. I saw Tom Bryar go into his faather's house and I followed him. I knew he would be confronting his faather about the rumours they were spreading about his wife," said John taking a deep breath. "After about five minutes I heard Bryar's daughter cry out and say mawther, they will kill faather. I went in the back door and saw Tom in a stooping position."

He paused and took another breath before continuing. "His faather, mawther and brother were all on him, beating him. Tom and his faather then went outside together, and I noticed that Tom looked exhausted, with his arm dangling down. There was a large patch of blood on his shoulder. His father had hold of him by the hair. John Oates came up and separated them, and then I helped John take Tom home to his house."

"What did you hear the prisoner say at his father's house on the seventeenth of December?"

John glanced at young Richard. "I said to him what a pity it was what he'd done to his brother. He said it ought to have been worse. I wish I had cut his head off."

"Thank you, Mr Symonds, you may step down," said Mr Hamilton. He flicked through several pages before looking up again. "I now call Mr John Oates."

John Oates took to the witness stand. Tom thought he looked even more nervous than he had been.

"Mr Oates, I believe you were present at Mr Bryar's house when Trooper Doyle came to collect the axe? Can you tell the court what you heard?"

"Aye. I heard the prisoner, Richard, talking to John Symonds. He said that it was not half bad enough and that he wished he'd cut his head off," said Oates looking nervously around the room. "I dunna know whose head he meant."

"Thank you, Mr Oates, you may return to your seat," said Mr Hamilton.

John Oates hurried back to his seat.

"I now call Doctor Croft."

Doctor Croft smiled at Tom as he passed by his seat on his way to the stand.

"Doctor Croft, I believe you attended to Mr Thomas Bryar that night. Would you please tell the court about the wound inflicted on him?"

"Of course. The wound was about four inches in length and extended down to the bone, which was splintered. I removed one splinter of bone, but believe there is another which will slough out over time."

"Has Mr Bryar been permanently injured?"

"I cannot say if the collar bone has been permanently injured. Mr Bryar will possibly get the use of his arm back when the splinter of bone comes away. I cannot say how long that may take."

"Is it possible that this wound was caused by an American axe used by a boy?"

"Yes I believe so," said Doctor Croft.

"Would it also be probable that it might have been done by an instrument with the blade up? Such as a drawing knife?"

"I wouldn't think that very likely," he replied.

"Thank you, Doctor Croft, you are excused," said Mr Hamilton. "Your Honor I have no further witnesses to call at this time."

"Very well," said Justice Gwynne. "This court will take a short recess, and will resume in one hour."

Tom and Jenni stood while the Magistrate and Jury left the courtroom. His mother and father managed to steal a few minutes with young Richard before he was taken away. Tom couldn't hear what they were saying, but he could see that his mother was crying. He sighed and turned away.

An hour later they were all called back into the court. Young Richard's solicitor Mr Ingleby stood up and called his first witness to the stand. "I call Mr Richard Bryar senior."

Tom's father walked calmly to the witness stand and faced the court. Tom swallowed hard. He wondered how his father would recall the events.

"Mr Bryar," said Mr Ingleby in a soft Scottish accent. "Would ye be so kind as to tell the court what your son, Mr Thomas Bryar, did when he arrived at your house on the evening of the fifteenth of December last?"

"Well, he came into my house and as he entered a young chap by the name of Dick Vivien was sitting at the door. And he says to him what have you got to say about my wife?" replied Richard calmly. "He said nothing. Tom then says to him I will haul your liver out, and as to you old man, I will haul your head off your shoulders."

"What were ye doing at the time Mr Bryar?"

"I was paring down the handle of my axe with a drawing-knife," said Richard. "Without saying another word to me he flew at me like a cat on a mouse and knocked me down. The young lad that was holding the handle of the axe got scared and escaped under his arm and out of the house."

"Then what happened?"

Richard took a breath before continuing. "After I was knocked down, my youngest son Richard came up. Tom grabbed him and began kicking him about the legs. Ye can still the marks he left."

"I see, so ye are saying that it was only after Mr Thomas Bryar threatened Mr Vivien and yourself, that your son Richard intervened?"

"Aye, that's right. There was a scuffle then that lasted for five or ten minutes, afore I threw Tom over onto the table," replied Richard. "Then Symonds came in and said hold him and I will help ye to kick the old bastard's guts out."

"Is that when your son Tom was wounded?"

"I dunna know. The table tilted up, and if he was cut it was probably because he hit his shoulder on the drawing-knife which was on the table."

There were several sniggers from the gallery.

Richard glanced around the courtroom. "I didna see any wound. Tom left the house in the same state as when he came."

"Thank ye, Mr Bryar that will be all," said Mr Ingleby.

Tom was furious, and it was only Jenni's hand on his arm that stopped him leaping to his feet. Surely the jury wouldn't believe such a pack of lies. He took several deep breaths and tried to calm himself, but it wasn't helping.

"Calm yourself, Tom," whispered Jenni. "They willna believe him."

"Tis a pack of lies that I left his house in one piece," hissed Tom.

"I know it, and the jury willna believe him. Ye must stay calm."

"Mr Richard Vivien to the stand please," said Mr Ingleby.

Dick Vivien was a young lad with a face full of freckles. He took his place at the stand and looked around the room wide-eyed and scared.

"Mr Vivien, did Mr Thomas Bryar threaten you and his father?"

"Aye," he replied nervously.

"Can ye tell the court, Mr Vivien, what occurred when young Mr Richard Bryar intervened?"

"Tom kicked him, and when he went to hit him his father took hold of him and threw him on the table. He broke a box of specimens and glass that was there."

"Is that when Mr Thomas Bryar was wounded?"

"I dunna know," he replied nervously glancing around the room.

"Do ye recall if the drawing-knife was lying on the table?"

"Aye, it was lying next to the axe handle."

"Thank ye, Mr Vivien that will be all for now," said Mr Ingleby. "I call Mrs Mary Bryar please."

Mary made her way cautiously to the witness stand. Mr Ingleby asked her several questions, and her testimony confirmed everything that Richard had said.

"How did your son appear to you when he left the house that evening?"

"He seemed fine to me."

"Thank ye Mrs Bryar you may step down," said Mr Ingleby. "I have no further witnesses to call Your Honor."

"Very well," said Justice Gwynne. "Mr Hamilton if you would like to address the jury."

"Thank you, Your Honor," said Mr Hamilton standing up. "It is a deplorable fact that a family should furnish such a serious case for enquiry, and that it should involve what I can only characterise as corrupt perjury. The evidence presented by the defence is so inconsistent that it is devoid of all credibility."

He took a deep breath and addressed the jury further. "The evidence is clear that Mr Thomas Bryar was attacked by his young brother with an axe. You have heard from witnesses that this was not enough. That he wished he had done further damage to his brother, perhaps to have even murdered him. In this case, there can only be one verdict. Guilty."

Mr Ingleby then addressed the jury as well. "Ye have heard from witnesses that when Mr Thomas Bryar left his father's house he was in fine form. There was no sign that he had been so injured. The only verdict you can return is one of not guilty."

"Thank you, gentlemen," said His Honor. "The jury will now deliberate their verdict."

The jurors stood and left the courtroom. Tom wondered how long they would deliberate. Although he was worried he would never be able to work again, he didn't wish his brother ill. What he couldn't reconcile were the lies his father had told about him. He had hoped that once the trial was over he'd make peace with his parents, but now that seemed impossible. How could he forgive their betrayal?

Half an hour later the court was reconvened and the jury returned. Tom didn't know what verdict he wanted. If his brother was found guilty he'd be sent to gaol, if not guilty, where would that leave him? He was so conflicted.

"Mr Johnson has the jury reached a unanimous verdict?" Justice Gwynne asked the head juror.

Mr Johnson rose to his feet. "Yes Your Honor," he replied. "We find the defendant guilty."

"Thank you, Mr Johnson. You and your fellow jurors have discharged your duty. You are dismissed."

Justice Gwynne waited while the jurors left the room and then he addressed young Richard. "It appears that your brother

Mr Thomas Bryar went to your father's house, in consequence of some libel on his wife. He conducted himself quietly, but your father came here, as the jury evidently thought, to give false account, and support it with perjury."

He paused and looked directly at his father. "Your father was strong enough to throw your brother onto a table, where he wished it to be inferred that he might have been cut by the implement lying there," said Justice Gwynne. "While there were several assaults upon the poor man, and he was helpless, you, with ferocity, took up an American axe and assailed your brother with it in a frightful manner."

He looked directly at young Richard. "When I heard your father swear palpable untruths and advance pretexts which only excited laughter in the jury box, I was compelled to conclude that you were both very wicked persons. It is the sentence of this court that you be imprisoned and kept to hard labour for the term of seven years."

Mary gasped and dissolved into loud sobs. Richard put his arm around his wife to comfort her and turned to look directly at Tom. The glare in his father's eyes told him everything he needed to know. There would be no reconciliation.

Justice Gwynne continued, as though he hadn't heard Mary's outburst. "The final week of that term is to be served in solitary confinement." He gathered his papers together and indicated to the clerk of courts.

"All stand for His Honor," said the Clerk of Courts rising to his feet.

Everyone stood and Justice Gwynne left the courtroom. The troopers then escorted young Richard from the room. He looked pale and scared and his eyes pleaded with his parents. Tom took a deep breath and looked away. He took no joy in his brother's misery.

Chapter 19

Moonta, April 1863

Life for Tom and Jenni would never be the same, Tom realised that. He was estranged from most of his family and couldn't imagine he would ever speak to his father again. His arm wasn't improving. He could move it from the elbow down, but his shoulder was frozen. He knew he'd never mine again, and just what he was going to do to support his family he didn't know. He despaired of ever being able to work again.

He still had most of the gold he'd exchanged to go to Newcastle back in November. There wasn't enough left to buy a house anywhere near the Wallaroo Mines, but houses were cheaper down the road in Moonta. He was anxious to move out of his old rented house and away from his parents. He constantly worried that Jenni would run into them and bear the brunt of their displeasure.

He purchased a modest house in East Terrace which took most of the money they had left. They managed to fill the house with second-hand furniture. It was shabby, but at least they had a roof over their heads.

By the end of April though it was becoming clear that they were in dire trouble. With no money coming in and no job in sight, Tom was left with no choice but to apply to the Destitute Board for relief. He was granted two months of food and firewood for himself and his family.

"What do we do when that runs out?" said Jenni wiping her hands on her apron. "We canna go on like this Tom."

"Dunna worry Jenni," he said taking her into his arms. "I swear I'll think of something." He had no idea what that would be, but he didn't want her to worry.

"I could take in laundry to help out?"

"You'll do no such thing. I promise ye I'll get a job doing something."

Two months later he was no closer to being employed and the charitable relief had run out. He couldn't stop Jenni from taking in laundry. It was hard back-breaking work and it broke his heart to see her reduced to such manual labour. He was determined to find some way to support his family. As the months went by, and still there was no hope of a job he sank into a deep depression. What use was a man if he couldn't care for and protect his family?

Over the next few months, there was no improvement in their situation. As winter dragged on so did Tom's gloomy outlook. He spent his days just sitting about the house in a state of apathy. Jenni despaired. She was working hard and doing her best to make ends meet, but she needed him to help. He needed to be useful, he needed a job.

It was early November when Jenni finally found what she thought was a solution to their predicament. While she was at the store she heard that old Jack Whitely had died. He'd been the town crier in Moonta for several years, and Jenni immediately thought of Tom. She couldn't wait to get home to tell him.

"Tom," she called as she came in the back door and put her shopping on the table. "Tom." She went through to the parlour and found him sleeping in his chair. God only knew what mischief Tommy and Marianne were up to.

"Tom," she said shaking him. "Wake up I have news."

"What. Aye," he said opening his eyes and blinking at her. "What's amiss? Are ye awright?"

"Aye, I'm fine. I've just come from the store, and I heard that old Jack Whitely died. Tom, ye could apply for his job as Town Crier. I know ye could do it."

He looked at her for several moments while the news sank in. "Town Crier, aye. Ah, Jenni, this could be the answer to our prayers," he said standing up looking at her. "Aye, I could do that."

"Of course ye could. I expect you'd have to apply down at the Institute in Wallaroo," she said smiling at him. "You'll need to bathe and clean yourself up a bit though."

He looked himself up and down and rubbed his fingers through his whiskers. She was right. His clothes were crumpled and stained. They looked like he'd been sleeping in them. He couldn't remember the last time he'd trimmed his beard.

"Aye," he smiled at her. "Thank ye, Jenni." He put his arms around her as best he could and kissed her. "Thank ye."

Tom felt more hopeful than he had in months. It was the best he'd felt since he was injured a year ago. Finally, he'd found a purpose, a job he could do to support his family. Not that the job of Town Crier paid that well. It was more or less a charitable position, but he thought he'd be able to handle all manner of announcements. He bathed and dressed in clean clothes before heading out the door.

"Wish me luck Jenni," he said kissing her.

"Ye dunna need luck, Tom," she said kissing him in return. "Just convince them that ye are the man for the job."

Jenni sighed as she watched him go down the street. She prayed he would be successful. If not then she didn't know what they were going to do.

.~.

Wallaroo, December 1863

Mary hurried down the street towards home. She'd been at Alice's for most of the day. She'd just announced she was expecting another bearn. After taking so long to have their first bearn, Emily who was born in May, Mary worried that it was too soon for her to be pregnant again. Her memory of losing Maryann eighteen months ago was still fresh in her mind.

She went in the back door and put her basket on the table. She sighed. She'd lost so much in the last couple of years. Not just Maryann, but it was ten months since she'd last seen Tom. She didn't want to think about young Richard. Every time her thoughts went there she came out in a cold sweat. The thought of him in gaol was almost too much for her to bear. She pushed all thoughts of him from her mind as she busied herself in the kitchen getting supper ready.

Christmas was fast approaching and she'd hoped by now Richard would've made peace with Tom. She missed her grandchildren something fierce, but every time she broached the subject with Richard, he just got angry.

"Do ye not understand Mary," he'd said the last time she'd raised the subject. "We went to court and lied to protect young Richard, but in doing so we lost Tom."

"But ye dunna know that Richard. If ye would explain it to him he'd understand. Please I miss them all so much. Will ye not make peace?"

"Can ye honestly say ye have forgiven that upstart Jenni? I haven't. Tis all her fault this happened in the first place."

Mary sucked in her breath. "No. But we must Richard. We must forgive and make peace."

"Tis too late," he'd shouted. "Dunna mention them again." He stormed out of the room and wouldn't discuss it any further.

She sighed. She knew Richard would be furious with her if she went behind his back. She'd considered doing it anyway on numerous occasions but was never quite brave enough. Maybe Alice could get through to him where she could not. She'd mentioned it to Alice today, but that hadn't gone well either.

"Faather willna thank me for interfering Ma, and ye knows it," Alice had said to her. "I'm sorry I canna help ye."

"But Alice your faather will listen to ye where he willna listen to me," she'd said. "Please, will ye not help me to get this family back together?"

Alice had hugged her and kissed her affectionately. "Ye know very well I would do anything for ye, but not this," she'd said more firmly. "Anyways, ye know I see Tom and Jenni from time to time, I dunna know if Da knows that, and he may not be happy if he found out. I canna risk it."

Mary had to concede that she was right on that point. Richard may not be too happy if he knew Alice had been sitting on the fence all this time. "Awright I willna ask ye again. But what am I to do Alice? Your faather willna budge and I miss Tom and my grandchildren so much."

Alice had not had any answers for her. Mary's heart ached for them, and she wiped a stray tear from her cheek as she peeled the potatoes for supper. She had to let it go. There was nothing she could do.

Chapter 20

Christmas 1864

Another year on and nothing much had changed for the Bryar family. Alice and George's son William was born in July. He was a fine healthy boy and Richard was delighted to have a new grandson. Alice had her hands full with four children now. Two under the age of two was proving to be a challenge.

Alice took Mary quietly aside to tell her that Tom and Jenni had also had another son. Phillip Bawden Bryar, they'd named him, and he was barely a month old.

"He's a gorgeous bearn with a mop of dark hair," said Alice getting the carving knife out of the drawer. "I think he looks a bit like Da."

Mary was glad of the news, but her heart ached for the grandson she would never see. "Are they well Alice? Tom and Jenni and the bearns. Are they doing awright?"

"Aye they're doing much better these days," replied Alice. "Ye know Tom is Town Crier now for Moonta, Wallaroo and

Kadina. It appears to suit him just fine. The bearns are all doing well. Ye wouldna recognise young Beth. She is so grown up."

Mary stirred the gravy while Alice began carving the goose for supper. "How I would love to see them," sighed Mary.

"Aye, of course, ye would. Da hasn't changed his mind?" enquired Alice as she began to slice the bird.

"No, and I daren't mention them again. The last time I tried to talk to him about making peace with Tom he got so angry. He willna talk about them."

Alice paused with her knife in the air. "Ma, have ye thought about going to see Tom without telling Da?"

"Aye of course I have," said Mary giving the gravy a vigorous stir. "But, your faather would never forgive me if he found out. I dare not."

Alice nodded in agreement as she went on carving the goose. "Aye, ye are right there. Well there is naught ye can do about it then," said Alice. "Ye are best forgetting about them."

"Ye are a mawther, ye know I canna do that," replied Mary astounded at her daughter's advice.

Alice put down her knife and wrapped her arm around her mother's shoulders. "I know, but I was just thinking about what would be best for ye Ma. I canna imagine what I would do if it was me."

"I hope ye never have to."

Five-year-old Mary came skipping into the kitchen. "Granfer wants to know when he's getting his supper?"

"Oh he must be getting hungry," said Mary smiling at her granddaughter. "It willna be very long. Can ye please tell Aunt Lizzie she's needed in the kitchen?"

"Aye Grammer," she said as she scampered out of the kitchen.

Alice finished carving the goose and piled roast vegetables onto the plates. The smells of roast meat and vegetables were making her stomach rumble. Lizzie helped carry the supper plates through to the dining room. Mary rounded up the children, and they all sat down to supper.

Richard gave thanks and Mary bowed her head and said her own prayers. It was the second Christmas she'd spent without young Richard and Tom at her table. She looked around at what remained of her family and sighed. She had to find the joy in what she had.

.~.

It was the beginning of autumn but there was no sign that the weather was cooling down. It had been a long hot dry summer, and Tom and Jenni had no water left in their rain tanks. It hadn't rained in nearly seven months and they now had no choice but to purchase distilled water. The price was getting ridiculously high. Tom was seriously considering their options.

"I know we've been doing awright with me working as Town Crier, but ye know my arm is so much better," said Tom flexing his arm to show her.

Jenni looked up from her sewing. "Aye, tis a lot better, but tis not strong enough for ye to go back mining if that's what ye are thinking."

"No I dunna think I could go back copper mining, but I reckon I could do something else."

"Something else, like what?" she enquired putting her sewing aside. "Tom, ye canna seriously think ye could use that arm all day."

"Maybe not, but I was thinking maybe I could get my own claim. I could work at my own pace."

Jenni couldn't help but notice the slight gleam of excitement in his eyes. "Awright. What are ye talking about?"

"Well I've heard there's been some new gold discoveries made around Clunes in Victoria," he said excitedly. "I reckon it would be just like mining copper, but I could do it by myself."

Victoria. Well, she had to agree that held some attraction. She'd heard it wasn't anywhere near as hot there, and she was really over the heat. They'd probably have plenty of water there as well. She didn't like the idea of having to pack and move, but she wasn't against the idea.

"Do ye seriously think ye could make a living at it?"

Tom leaned forward in his chair and looked into his wife's curious face. "Aye I do," he said. "We'll never get ahead here. There's not much else I can do. But, who knows what opportunities there might be on the goldfields. What do ye say, Jenni?"

Jenni smiled at him. "Ye know very well I will follow ye to the ends of the earth. I have done," she said. "If ye wants to give it a try, then I'll come with ye."

He leapt out of his chair and grabbed her in a hug. "Thank ye, Jenni. I'm only just thinking on it. I haven't decided for sure if we should do it. But tis good to know ye will come with me."

A squawk from the bedroom indicated that Phillip was awake and hungry. Jenni let her husband go and started towards the bedroom.

"There is just one condition Thomas Bryar," she said over her shoulder. "We will pay all our debts afore we leave."

Tom laughed. "Aye."

Over the next few months, the idea of leaving the peninsular for the cooler climes of Clunes took hold. Tom was convinced he could make a go of it. It was a risk, but he knew he wouldn't be happy being Town Crier for the rest of his life. He was a miner, and if it wasn't copper, then why not gold.

.~.

Wallaroo, August 1865

Richard lay back down on the bed feeling exhausted while Doctor Croft fossicked in his bag. He had never felt so weak in his entire life, and the incessant coughing was only weakening him further. It had all started with what he thought was a cold. He'd had a sore throat and a slight cough a week ago, which he hadn't been too concerned about. Now the coughing had gotten so bad he could barely catch his breath. His lungs had never been the same since the fire in the Burra Mine.

"What do ye think Doc?" he croaked in between coughs.

"Dunna speak Richard," said Mary coming to his bedside. "Ye need to keep your strength up."

"Well I don't think it's diphtheria," replied Doctor Croft retrieving a small jar from his bag. "I believe you may have the pneumonia in your right lung. I recommend bed rest and the main thing is to keep warm Mr Bryar."

He put the small jar on the side table. "Use this to make a tincture Mrs Bryar. Steep it in his tea, and have him take it three times a day. It's willow bark and it will help to reduce the inflammation. Some clear broth will also assist, and I'll come by and check on you in a day or two," he said snapping his bag closed.

"Oh thank ye, Doctor Croft," said Mary inspecting the small brown jar. "Would it also help him to inhale some vapours?"

"It may do, but no more than once a day," he replied picking up his bag. "I expect you'll be feeling better in a day or two as long as you rest."

Mary kept a vigilant watch on him over the next few days, but his condition didn't appear to be getting any better. He had no energy and just lay in bed exhausted. He complained of chest pains every time he coughed, and Mary feared his condition was worsening. By the third day, his breathing was so laboured and difficult that she went for the doctor again.

Doctor Croft came late in the day to see him. He listened to his chest and gave him a thorough examination. Richard was wracked with fever and he was hot and clammy to the touch.

"I'm afraid the infection's spread to the other lung," said Doctor Croft. "Continue the willow bark tea and bed rest."

"Will he be awright Doctor?" asked Mary as she helped Richard to lie back down.

"I'm afraid it will have to run its course Mrs Bryar, but I believe a chest rub may help." He opened his bag and took out a vial of camphor oil. He unbuttoned Richard's shirt and rubbed it vigorously onto his chest. "This should help to relieve the congestion."

He handed the vial to Mary. "Rub it onto his chest twice a day," he said. "I'll come by and check on you tomorrow Mr Bryar."

"Thank ye," Richard whispered hoarsely. It was all he could manage before closing his eyes and sighing.

Doctor Croft came by to check on Richard every day for the next week. Mary was doing everything possible, but there was no improvement.

Doctor Croft closed his bag and indicated that Mary should follow him from the room. Mary gave Richard one last pat to make sure he was tucked warmly in bed before following the Doctor into the parlour.

"Mrs Bryar I'm sure you've realised your husband isn't improving," said Doctor Croft when they were alone in the parlour. "I've done all I can, but you must prepare yourself. Your husband may not recover." He reached out and squeezed her arm. "I'm sorry."

"What do ye mean I must prepare myself?" said Mary alarmed by the doctor's tone. "Are ye suggesting he might die?"

"I'm afraid I've seen these cases before Mrs Bryar. He is not responding to treatment, and there is nothing more I can do for him," he replied. "He's not likely to last more than a few days."

"Surely there must be something more that can be done?" said Mary. She knew he wasn't getting better as quickly as she'd expected, but she hadn't considered that he might not recover. Tears pricked her eyes and she sucked in her breath. "Please Doctor Croft, ye must help him."

"I'm sorry Mrs Bryar," he replied picking up his bag. "I'll call again tomorrow. Good day." He opened the door and stepped out without another word.

Mary followed him out onto the front porch. "Doctor Croft I beg ye. Please," she implored him. She blinked back her tears as she looked expectantly at the doctor.

He turned to face her. "I'm sorry Mrs Bryar. There's nothing more I can do. You must believe me, I would do more if I could."

She watched him go down the street while trying to comprehend the fact that she might lose Richard. She felt numb and allowed her tears to finally fall. She sat down on the front porch and allowed her fears to take over. She wasn't sure how long she'd sat there crying, but the cold seeping into her bones finally brought her to her senses. She was freezing cold and shivered as she got to her feet and went inside. What was she going to do if anything happened to Richard?

Three days later she was faced with her worst fears. She'd been sleeping in the spare room with Lizzie so as not to disturb Richard. She went into the room they'd shared with a hot cup of tea for him. He looked like he was still asleep.

"Richard come on, I've brought ye a nice hot cup of tea," she said shaking him. He didn't respond. She put the tea down and shook him hard with both hands. "Richard," she yelled at him.

She stared at him and then felt for his pulse before she convinced herself that he'd died in his sleep. She slumped on top of him and hugged him as she cried and called his name over and over.

It was Lizzie who on hearing her mother's calls went into the room. It was a pitiful sight, and her breath caught in her throat. Her father had died in the night, and her mother was clinging to him and chanting his name.

She went to her mother and put her arms around her. "Oh, Ma."

She didn't acknowledge her daughter's presence. She was too distraught to take in anything other than the fact that Richard was gone. She cried and clung to him ignoring everything else.

The next week was a blur for Mary. She went through the motions of life without really noticing. She had Richard laid out for viewing in the parlour dressed in his Sunday best. Her son-in-law George took care of the burial at the Kadina

Cemetery following a service conducted at home by the Reverend. It was all over before the reality of losing her husband had really dawned on her.

She had some money coming in a few weeks from the current mining contract that Richard had been working on. She had no idea what she was going to do when that ran out. They had a few pounds in the bank, but not enough for her to live on for any length of time. She had no idea what she was going to do. She couldn't seem to wrap her mind around it.

Chapter 21

Moonta, September 1865

Tom walked down the street towards home, very satisfied with his day's work. He felt lighter than he had in months, the anxiety that had been plaguing him was almost gone. He'd spent the last hour or so down at the Port of Wallaroo arranging for transport on one of the coastal vessels. He was pleased with the deal he'd struck. They would be sailing for Melbourne in two weeks onboard the Melville. He was so excited at the prospect of finally making the move to Clunes.

They'd sold the house, and he wasn't concerned about the furniture. It was all second hand and not worth enough to worry about. His only concern was that the money from the sale of their house wouldn't come through until after they'd departed. He was sure he could count on his brother-in-law to forward the proceeds onto him once they were settled.

He was grinning from ear to ear when he arrived home, and couldn't wait to share his news with Jenni. He was surprised to find his brother-in-law George was visiting. He and Jenni were sitting at the kitchen table.

"George, nice to see ye," said Tom slapping him on the back as he passed. "To what do we owe the pleasure?" He checked the teapot before pouring himself a cup and sitting down at the table.

Jenni gave him an odd sideways glance. "George has come with some news."

"Ah, that's right," said George clearing his throat.

"News. What news do ye have George? Dunna tell me ye and Alice are expecting another bearn? I must say ye dunna waste any time," said Tom smiling at him.

"Ah no. Well, not as far as I know," said George appearing to choose his words carefully. "No, I'm afraid tis not good news, Tom. Tis your Da."

"My Da? What's amiss then?"

"Well, he took very ill with the pneumonia a while back," replied George. "Anyways, he wasna getting better and well..." He paused and swallowed. "I'm ever so sorry to have to tell ye Tom, but he died last week."

"What? He died?" He had certainly not expected his father might die anytime soon, and he was shocked at the news.

"Aye. I took care of his funeral myself. I thought your mawther might have told ye afore he was buried, but obviously, she didn't. Alice thought ye ought to know."

"Aye, well I thank ye for telling me, George. But I can hardly believe it," said Tom shaking his head. "I always thought we'd make peace afore he died. I guess that isna going to happen now."

"Perhaps ye should go and see your mawther?" said Jenni pressing her lips together. "Tis not too late to make amends with her."

Tom grimaced. "No, tis too late for that. If she couldna even come to tell me that my own faather had died, I have nothing to say to her."

Jenni couldn't help but hear the bitterness in his voice. She reached out and put her hand on his. "Tom, dunna say such things. Tis never too late."

He squeezed her hand and looked into her soft grey eyes. "Well, in this case, it is. I booked us passage for Melbourne. We leave in two weeks. I came straight home from the Port as I couldna wait to tell ye."

"Oh Tom that's wonderful," she said smiling at him. "We willna have to find somewhere else to live afore we leave."

"So ye are really leaving then?" put in George. "I know Alice will be sad to see ye go, but we understand and wish ye all the best."

"Thank ye, George," said Tom. "I've a favour to ask of ye. The money from the house willna be paid until after we've gone. Would ye take care of it and send it to us once we've got settled in Clunes?"

"Of course, Tom. I'm glad I can be of some help to ye."

"I appreciate it, George. We'll write you as soon as we're settled."

"What about your mawther Tom?" said Jenni looking concerned. She was determined that he should make peace with her before they leave. "Ye must go and see her afore we leave at least."

Tom sighed and looked at his wife. He knew she wouldn't let up until she'd got her way, but he really couldn't see the point. It had been two and a half years since he'd spoken to his mother and in all that time she'd made no attempt to make peace with him. She'd backed his father when he'd lied about him in court. What was he supposed to say to her?

"I'll think about it."

Jenni smiled at him, but he knew that look and groaned inwardly. No doubt as soon as George had left she would continue to badger him.

They were so busy over the following week that all thoughts of his mother were forgotten. They packed what household goods they could fit into the sea trunk. Clothes and blankets had to fit into another chest, and Tom's tools and boots in another. Some things would just have to be left behind, but Tom wasn't concerned. They'd come all the way from England with very little and they'd managed. He was sure that they'd be able to make do again.

It was a couple of days before they were due to leave when Jenni mentioned his mother again.

"Tom I know ye are still hurt, but your mawther has lost her husband. I hate to think how she must be feeling," said Jenni folding the towels she was packing. "Will ye at least go and tell her that we are leaving? I hate the idea of us just going without saying a word to her."

Tom groaned. "I dunna know what I'd say to her Jenni. It's been too long, and I'd rather just go."

"Please Tom. If not for yourself, do it for the bearns. Ye know one day they're going to ask about her, and it would be nice if ye could tell them that ye said goodbye." She put the towel into the chest and wrapped her arms around him in a warm hug. "I think ye really need to do this."

"Awright, I'll go and see her," he replied hugging her close. "I'll go to keep the peace with ye, for no other reason."

.~.

Tom took a deep breath and tried to calm himself. His heart was hammering in his chest and he had an overwhelming desire to turn and run. The last time he'd been outside this house he'd been bleeding profusely and knocked senseless. The memory of that night came flooding back and he almost turned on his heel. He forced himself to walk up the path to the front door. He swallowed and took several more deep breaths and knocked on the door.

Time seemed to stand still while he waited on the doorstep. It was no more than a minute when the door opened. He found himself looking into his mother's dark brown eyes. She was older than he remembered and her once unruly auburn hair was now a salt and pepper grey.

"Tom," she said clearly surprised to find her eldest son standing on her porch.

"Ma," he said sucking in his breath. "I ah....I've come to say goodbye. Jenni and I are leaving for Victoria. So goodbye." What else could he say? He hadn't expected to feel as detached as he did. The woman standing before him was his mother for God's sake.

"Tom, I'm ever so sorry," she said reaching out a hand to touch him. "I have missed ye so much. Won't ye come in?" She stepped aside and invited him to come inside.

He looked at her blankly for a moment. "No. Goodbye Ma." He turned and started to walk back down the path.

Mary ran after him. "Please Tom ye must come in. I can explain everything. I've wanted to come and see ye for ever so long, but your faather wouldna allow it. Please let me explain."

He paused for a moment and resisted the urge to turn and face her. No - It was all too late. Without a backwards look, he continued down the path and out onto the street. His heart was still hammering in his chest and he felt as nervous as a boy, but he walked on.

"Tom. Tom, please we had to try to save young Richard. We couldna help ye," said Mary following him down the path.

He stopped. "Stop Mawther. I dunna want to hear it. Goodbye." He hurried down the street and tried to block out the sound of his mother calling his name.

Chapter 22

Mary's heart was pounding as she walked down the street. She clutched Alice's arm and sucked in a deep breath. What if Tom wouldn't let her in? She'd spent last night agonising over today's visit. If Alice hadn't agreed to accompany her she would've been too afraid.

As it was she was terrified he'd turn her away, but she'd lost too much to leave words unsaid any longer. Even if this was the last time she saw him, she was determined to make peace. Alice stopped outside a small run-down timber house. The garden was unkept and the paint was peeling off the weatherboards. Mary's heart ached at the sight of it. Tom and Jenni had such a lovely home in Hughes Street.

"Are ye ready Ma?" said Alice giving her mother a reassuring smile.

Mary nodded but remained stationary as she stared at the house. Her heart was beating so fast she thought it'd jump right out of her chest. She took a breath and let go of Alice's arm.

She nodded again. "Aye, I'm ready."

She walked up the worn dirt path and taking another deep breath, knocked on the door. She came out in a cold sweat as she stood there waiting. If Alice hadn't been at the bottom of the path she'd have bolted. The door opened.

"Mary."

"Hello, Jenni. I wonder if I could see Tom? Is he home?" said Mary licking her lips as she eyed her daughter in law. She didn't know what she'd do if she slammed the door in her face. She tried to give her a warm smile, but her skin felt stretched and unnatural and she feared it came across as a sneer.

"Aye of course," she replied stepping aside.

"Thank ye," said Mary as she stepped into the parlour.

It was obvious they would be leaving soon. A large sea trunk stood in the middle of the floor, along with a smaller chest against the wall. Folded clothes were sitting on the sofa ready to go into the waiting chest. Peering into the trunk Mary saw that Tom's tools were already packed.

"Grammer," said Beth coming into the parlour and catching sight of her grandmother. She stared from Mary to her mother, indecision clear on her young face.

Mary's breath caught in her throat at the sight of her eldest granddaughter. She'd grown so much since she last seen her, and her eyes clouded with tears.

"Beth," she said looking first at Beth and then at Jenni, who gave her the slightest nod. She opened her arms wide and approached her. Beth threw herself into her arms and the two of them hugged each other tightly. Mary kissed her and sobbed from the sheer joy of holding her once more. "Oh, my darling I've missed ye so much."

"I've missed ye like mad," said Beth wiping tears from her eyes. "I canna believe ye are here."

Mary smiled at her through her tears and cupped her face in her hand. "I know, and I canna tell ye how sorry I am that it's been so long."

The sound of children's voices could be heard coming down the hall, and a moment later they filled the doorway. Susan was the first to run forward and grab her grandmother in a tight hug.

"Grammer," said Esther joining her older sisters.

Mary wrapped her arms around the three of them and rained kisses on them. "Oh my sweethearts," she said as she clung to them.

The three youngest children peered at Mary from the doorway. Five-year-old Tommy stared at her before running to his mother. He grabbed hold of her skirt and peered at Mary.

"Come girls, give the littlies a chance to say hello," said Jenni smiling through her unshed tears. "Ye remember Grammer?" she said to Tommy.

He nodded but remained firmly attached to her skirt.

Mary extracted herself and approached Tommy. Getting down on her knees she smiled. "Do ye have a hug for me?"

He nodded, and after hesitating for another moment, wrapped his arms around her neck. "Grammer."

"Oh Tommy I have missed ye," said Mary hugging him close. "My, how ye've grown."

"This is Marianne and Phillip," said Jenni leading her youngest daughter over to Mary. She placed Phillip in her arms. He immediately began screeching and wriggling to be free. Mary laughed, and after giving him several kisses let him go. He crawled away from her before sitting and staring from a safe distance.

Three-year-old Marianne gave her a shy hug before retreating as well. Mary sighed as she got to her feet. Her heart was fit to burst from sheer joy and she wiped her tears of happiness away with the back of her hand.

"Thank ye, Jenni. I dunna deserve such kindness from ye," she said taking a deep breath.

"Nonsense, Mary," said Jenni taking her into her embrace. "I'm only sorry it's taken so long. I wish we could've made peace years ago."

"I know," said Mary stepping back. "Richard wouldna allow it. And I'm so sorry I didn't go behind his back, but I was afeared to."

"Have ye seen my..," said Tom coming to halt in the doorway. He stared at his mother surrounded by his wife and children. He sucked in a breath and slowly let it out. "Mawther."

"Come," said Jenni scooping Phillip into her arms. "Let's leave ye faather and Grammer to talk." She shooed the children ahead of her as they left the parlour.

Mary pressed her lips together and eyed her son warily. She was determined to have her say and have peace with her family.

"I will have peace between us," she said. Her breast was heaving as her heart thumped madly. "Please dunna ask me to leave until I've said what I need to say."

Tom stared at her for a moment. "Did Alice tell ye where to find us?"

"Aye. She came with me, she's outside."

Tom opened the door and peered outside. "Come in, Alice," he said stepping aside to allow her to enter. "I willna have ye standing out there. Jenni would love to see ye I'm sure."

"Thank ye," she said giving her mother a sideways glance as she entered. She gave her brother a peck on the cheek before heading down the hall to the kitchen.

Tom watched her go before turning to face his mother. "Awright. Say it, and then ye will leave."

Mary licked her lips. "It was ye faather's idea," she said dropping her gaze from his. "He didna think we could do anything to help ye. The damage was already done."

"Aye, well he was right about that," said Tom dispassionately.

Mary nodded and sucked in a deep breath. She slowly let it out before going on. "Your Da thought we might be able to save young Richard from going to gaol. That's why he lied to the judge," she said eyeing him. "We thought we'd be able to make peace with ye later."

Tom stared at her for a moment. The tension in his shoulders eased as he allowed them to slump. "So what happened? Why did ye not make peace with me?"

Mary's breathing eased slightly. If Tom was interested enough to ask questions there was hope. "Your faather was hurt and angry," she said pressing her lips together. "He thought it was a family matter, and that ye didna have to involve the police."

Tom ran his fingers through his hair and grimaced. "Aye, I didna want to...not really. I thought it was Da that had attacked me. It was only later that I realised it was young Richard. I didna want him to go to gaol, but there was naught I could do."

Mary nodded. She understood perfectly that it was out of his hands, but Richard hadn't agreed. "So, when young Richard was sent to gaol your faather was angry. Angry at you, and all thoughts of making peace with ye went out the window." She sighed and looked earnestly into her son's face. "I wanted to see ye so bad, but your Da wouldn't allow it, and I was afeared to go behind his back."

Tom's eyes clouded over and he nodded. Several seconds ticked by before he said anything. "Why did ye not come and tell me he was dead? I would've come and said my goodbyes at least."

"Aye, I'm sorry about that. I wasn't myself ye understand. I was grief-stricken and I wasna thinking straight." She took a step closer to him and looked into his eyes, glistening with unshed tears. "Please, Tom. Can we not put this behind us? Ye are my son and I love ye, and I would have peace afore I die."

He stared at her and his face softened. "I forgave ye a long time ago," he said barely above a whisper.

Mary heaved a sigh and gave him a tremulous smile as fresh tears ran down her cheeks. "It's more than I deserve."

He nodded. "We leave for Clunes in two days, and we willna be back," he said with finality. "I willna have ye on my conscious, so ye may stay and spend time with the bearns."

"Thank ye," she said looking deep into his face. He was unmoving, and although he'd offered words of forgiveness, she wanted more. She took a step closer and held out her arms. "I'm so sorry Tom."

She saw his resolve was crumbling. He looked at for a moment, before running this thumb across her cheeks to wipe away her tears. "I'm sorry to Ma." He pressed his lips together and engulfed her in his arms.

Mary clung to him and sobbed as she buried her face in his shoulder. Their tears intermingled as mother and son let go of the lies and resentment that had kept them apart for so long.

The End

Author Notes

Thank you so much for reading my book. I'm an Australian indie author. As such, I maintain complete control of my work and self publish. That also means I have to market and promote my work, which I'm not very good at. I find it hard to self promote.

So, I'm taking this opportunity to not only thank you for taking the time to read my book, but if you liked it, would you mind leaving a rating or review on Amazon. It's the best way to show any author that you appreciate their hard work. It also helps other potential readers to decide if they should invest their time and money.

You already know that I write historical fiction, and you may have also realised that my stories are based on the lives of my ancestors. I've been passionate about family history for many years, and I've discovered so many amazing ancestors who led such interesting lives. So, I blend fact with fiction and bring their stories to life, and I'm so excited to be sharing them with you.

If you enjoyed this book, please consider reading one of my other titles.

Thank you

Jacob's Mob

Delve into a little unknown Australian history...

It's 1825 on the Hunter River in a small place called Wallis Plains. Large parcels of land have been granted to the wealthy and retired, who have been assigned convicts to work that land. Vicars Jacob is one such man. Retired from the East India Company he's been granted two thousand acres on the Hunter River and assigned twenty convicts. One of his convicts, Patrick Riley, lost four of his sheep and was sentenced to receive fifty lashes. On the way to Newcastle, he escapes and returns to Jacob's property. Lawrie Clearly and Aaron Price join him and they terrorise Jacob's Overseer before stealing food and going bush. More absconded convicts join them and they soon become known as Jacob's Mob.

For months they terrorised the settlers of Wallis Plains, seeking revenge and breaking into their houses, even setting them on fire. Magistrate, Alexander Scott is determined to hunt them down and bring them to justice. Can he find them before they escape to America where the British have no jurisdiction? Or can he bring them to justice...

Based on the true story of The Jacob's Mob.

Margaret

From Bredgar House to Van Diemen's Land.....

Margaret Chambers never imagined she'd be forced to flee her family home and country to escape a hideous old man and an arranged marriage. Pretending to be a general servant she boards a ship bound for Hobart Town. It's 1837, and in order to get free passage out to Van Diemen's Land, she's agreed to work for Mrs Hector. There's just one problem, she's never done a day's menial work in her life and her lie is soon discovered.

Taken into the household of the Reverend Davies and his wife Maria, she not only finds kindness but friendship, and is employed as Maria's companion. She couldn't have hoped for a better situation, but when convict and scoundrel William Hartley crosses her path will it all come tumbling down? Seduced by the young and charming William she finds herself unable to remain with the Reverend and his wife.

Maria doesn't want her to go but Margaret can see the conflict between Maria and her husband. Not wanting to be the cause of any rift between them she leaves.

William still has five years of his seven-year sentence to serve and he's not free to marry her. However, he stands by her side by stealing food for her and his unborn child until he gets caught. Sent away to work on the chain gang Margaret's left to fend for herself. Somehow she finds a way to survive until William's free to join her and when he gets a Ticket of Leave and permission to marry her, the future's looking hopeful.

Printed in Great Britain
by Amazon